I0547204

Copyright © 2022 by K. N. Robertson
Published in 2022 by Kush Books LLC
Cover and book design by Kozakura

The characters and events in this book are fictitious.
Any similarities to real persons, living or dead, is coincidental and not intended by the author.

Printed in the United States of America

First edition: 2022
ISBN 979-8-9860827-1-4
Fiction / Fantasy / General

Version 1

CIP data for this book is available from the library of congress

KNRobertson.com

EXPOSING
LESSER DEMONS

THIS IS THE SECOND COMING
OF THE SUPERNATURAL.

K. N. ROBERTSON

Kush Books

Not Into Temptation, but...

Friday:

Deana did not intend to seduce her psychiatrist. Still, the poised older woman sat before her tempted. The hour was almost up, and Deana spent it stalling until the last possible second, blathering on about once seemingly unattainable goals she had managed to achieve recently. Thinking nothing of it, she lay back on the chaise, eyeing the clock while the doctor eyed her.

Until then, there was a sense of glaring pride between the two of them, but a new and intense feeling struck, then slithered hastily away. Deana hardly sensed it but was able to empathize. In her mind she termed it, *temptation*.

She followed the doctor's lead, ignoring the rogue feeling. Instead, intending to satisfy the more harmless curiosity that remained. There was barely enough time for Deana's, now expected, last minute, startling revelation. "I found him." She said feigning innocence.

"Who?" There was a pulse of genuine curiosity about before the disappointment of realization.

Deana admitted, "My ex, Laz."

"The one you called a monster?" Dr. Michelle Stevens asked with a condemning tone. She knew the name well. She knew all of Deana's exes by name.

"That was before I knew monsters were real," She deflected.

"Is that what you think of them? That they're monsters?"

"No." She cringed regretting her statement instantly. "Of course not. Some of them are almost... normal. You'd never know."

"You mean the psychics and such, right?"

"Right. You know, I even think I might be one."

"A psychic?" Dr. Steven's raised an eyebrow.

"Or something... Maybe."

"What would you say is your ability?" Dr. Stevens asked pen hovering over her clipboard.

"Empathy. Like, super empathy."

"Oh? I thought that was my job," She chuckled at herself, and Deana did not sense any of the expected heavy emotions from either confession. The doctor continued, smiling, "Can you tell what I'm feeling now?"

"Maybe." Deana blushed. "Sometimes, I can identify when the feeling in the room changes, but usually it's hard to tell... I can't always make a clear distinction between your feelings and mine." There was a pause between them as Deana tried to assign the current adoration in the room to its rightful owner.

Dr. Stevens smiled and dropped her head unable to look her patient in the eye. She annotated something then changed the subject. "I'm sorry, I still don't understand your earlier statement,

Deana. You're clean now, safe, thriving, not one panic attack in months... Why look for Laz? After so many positive changes?"

Deana spoke carefully. "It was easy to make Laz seem like the only bad guy after we ended."

"His actions made that easy." Dr. Stevens corrected.

"Right, but... I still have amends to make. Like, maybe I haven't been so honest with him about some pretty important things." Deana hoped Stevens would not ask for details. When she did not, Deana continued, "I thought about writing a message that I'd never send, tried writing one that I would send, and in the end, I always feel like there are things I have to say to his face. Anything less feels... unfair. I can't do that, even to him... So, I asked him to dinner."

"Must be pretty important for you to face someone who's put you through so much."

"It is, and I have to confront my worst fears soon anyway, scarier things than him."

"And you think confronting him is a start." Stevens sat back thoughtfully, "I can understand that. Sometimes it's good for people to face the person who's made them feel victimized, but Deana, I can't imagine what you'd have to face that would be harder for you than that. You said once, it felt like he was hypnotizing you, and considering recent events, I can't help but think he may have been. Are you sure you're ready to see him again?"

She thought for a moment. "I have to. I... I just *have* to. It feels like I can't go one more step with my life until I get this done." Before Doctor Stevens questioned her vague statement Deana tried with a fake calmness to reassure her. "Besides, I have my power. I'll know if he starts to get on edge, although I wish I had something like the others, The Anomalous. Something defensive I could fight with... just in case.

"But I won't fall for him again... I don't miss him, not like that. That's one addiction I can say I have completely recovered from. And yet, I haven't been... intimate with anyone in a while. not since..."

"... Parker." The doctor finished.

"And I'm not quite over Parker... or ready to talk about them. And I really need to... you know."

Stevens smiled. "I know."

The feeling changed in the room again. "Laz wouldn't be the worst I could do in that department... if it could just be one night."

"Being intimate with an ex can bring up unresolved issues." Dr Stevens cautioned. Deana sat up, contemplating. Dr. Stevens continued, "And a lot of people are more dangerous now. He could be too."

"Yet, *he's* never drugged me without my consent."

"True, I guess you won't have to worry about Rezestra with him."

"Or any other drugs, so he says." Deana thought back to her chat with Laz, "Supposedly he's clean now too."

"Do you think he has a power... That he is one who may have

always had a power?"

"Well," she smirked, "he always did have me under his spell."

Higher Authority

Thursday (the night before):

Laz could tell he was playing with a dead body from the moment his consciousness divided and entered the places its soul left. He found the John doe slumped in the alley while looking for something to curb his craving. He dipped into the soulless hollow places. They reached and embraced him as something new and, though incomplete, in total control.

He could remember the prophetess cooing to him as he trembled from withdrawal like it was only yesterday. "Magic started your addiction. It can help you manage it."

So, Laz spoke to the corpse. His words became a command, "Make sure you're found." In his mind, he envisioned the place he wanted the corpse to go. Images of a nearby precinct flowed from him and electrified the corpse into some less-than-half-alive state of being. The body pulled itself onto begrudging legs and trudged to the station before it collapsed on the tile stinking of days unwashed and hours cold.

It was an easy thing to get the dead body to the police station, easier than persuading the living killer to turn themselves in. Those who used were easy to move and provided a fix he could experience while staying clean himself, technically. Now and again, he used junkies to drive away more than just his desire to expand his abilities. Yet it was the dead that were sure to give Laz all the neural pleasure of flexing his greatest talent with none of the hangovers from fighting the resistant mind of a living and thinking being.

Before Laz could reassemble his consciousness, he heard the jarring, far-off honk of a car horn. He craned his head to listen to the commotion in the distance. He had intended for tonight's hunt to be a mental exercise, not physical, but barely himself, his body lurched into action. He jogged uphill toward the bridge stumbling, mind still buzzing from winding up the corpse. He ran with stalled traffic on one side of him, the river on the other, and only a few feet of steel keeping him out of both.

Water crashing against boulders relaxed him in the chaos and lured him steadily along the bridge until he could hear and absorb a single voice screaming to a crowd.

"Get back! I have powers and I'll use them!" Yelled a potential jumper, brandishing empty hands. The man was intoxicated, Laz discovered, as he wobbled with a drunk sway. However, the man's decision seemed to be firmly in place, "Just let me die in peace! Go away!"

Sirens wailed in the distance, but no emergency help was currently present. Laz rejoiced at the rare opportunity. Except on TV, he had not seen another mage in months. Not since The Madam banished him from their private Eden without a single contact on the outside. Much as he liked practicing on the dead, he missed the rich inner world of an experienced mage. There was just enough time to probe the mind of this one and try to make him change his decision before help arrived or he hit the water.

Laz stepped a few feet back into the gathering crowd, enough to detach himself from the scene as far as any witness could tell. For support, he leaned against a truck that was pulled over on the shoulder.

He concentrated on the man, and for a second heard only his

shouting while the other voices faded to a quiet static. He then focused on the dull aura that surrounded the mage's body. Laz pushed his mental presence into the befuddled mind. The man's ranting faded to a mumble as his mind accepted the invasion. Through their mental link he began to communicate with Laz, sharing only semi-conscious thoughts. Laz dug into deeper levels of the man's awareness without much resistance as he could only do with the inebriated and unconscious. The man was drunk enough to invite Laz or any other entities to flow into him.

Laz began to look for reasons this soul should live and found himself lacking in happy memories, but he could see pain clear as day. The man loathed himself, a once-neglected child forced to be alone and scared while others praised him for his independence. Now grown, he lived a lonely existence, unable to communicate his affection and unable to accept it from others. He hated his job but he, like his parents before him, had debts to pay for acquired "assets." Like his parents, he satisfied social expectations of owning a practical car and paying monthly on a nice house near good schools. Yet unlike them he had no children to send to these prestigious institutions. Also, unlike them, no lover to speak of. The man was a normal bachelor, with normal childhood trauma and pain. Laz felt the man's pain, empathized even, but this man was lying about his magic. There was none and that made him afraid to exist.

Laz had newfound reasons for not wanting the man to jump. He implanted the suggestion not to in the man's mind. He craved a reason to live. It should have been easy to make him resist, but his mind had long since been made up. He had pondered the reasons to let go for so long that Laz felt he was buried under them as he scavenged for one memory of love or joy or lasting friendship within his mind.

The man – Vern, feared mages and wanted to become one to protect himself or be free from them entirely. Laz could not imagine living in this substantial fear and loathing alone and powerless. Neither could Vern. He chose to take death into his own hands. Yet, here Death was, trying like hell to keep him alive.

Some part of the man noticed Laz's presence interfering with his thoughts. Vern began to fight him back internally; the conflicting ideas tearing him apart. He yelped and begged, rejecting Laz's attempts to suggest he live, believing the ideas to be his own false hopes. Unknowingly, Vern purged his many reasons of wanting to let go for Laz to see. Consciously tortured at the remembrances, he sobbed.

Laz discerned a warm, copper light gravitating toward him from the darkness of Vern's mind.

Laz reached for the warmth as he was pulled into a memory. He observed the neglected child Vern once was, crying in tandem with the man of today. He attempted to soothe himself, and as he shuddered, the copper light expanded, shining unyielding, their attention brought back to the present moment.

Laz tried once more to coax Vern to come down, again he resisted, reviewing his reasons once again. He flipped through memories of the empty mortgaged house where he saw himself dying bored and alone at best. He had imagined his porch with months of Sunday papers before anyone came to check on him. The man yelled and cried loudly in reaction to memories and fears of the future. The light narrowed and Vern had reached his wits end. He could not allow that future to be his fate. He jumped.

In his mind's eye, Laz grabbed for the constricting copper light and pulled, taming the light back to him, filling the dim space with its now blinding warmth. But it was too late, Vern was in the water surrendering to its power.

'Live!' Laz begged. He desperately implanted thoughts of hope, but the man believed that his peace was from having jumped. He thought it came from the suffocating and drowning that began as he was drifting nearer to death.

Laz had never been in someone's head as they died. After they died of course, even before, but he would always be gone before the great change was completed. This time he intended to stay and feel his failure. Learn from it like all the others in his life.

"Focus on the states between life and death," he remembered being taught not long ago, so he did.

The copper light remained, but began to divide itself into sections, smaller and smaller, they bubbled and separated until they were so small, they appeared as tiny grains of sand. Suddenly, Laz felt... Life. Vern was alive! He felt Vern's surprise, confusion, and finally, hope.

Laz wished he could see the man. However, Vern was suddenly delighted as he compared himself to dolphins, whales, and jellyfish. Laz borrowed the man's vision and could see himself submerged into the littered river under the bridge, rocky and muddy brown. He had seen it with more joy and light than ever.

'You're a merman.' Laz transmitted in amazement. Vern was alive. Evolved, albeit scaly. A once ordinary human now magical.

Laz returned to himself tired from his work as the cries of spectators began to shift from sadness to awe for Vern's transformation. Although he did not have powers until Laz unearthed them, he pretended to. He made threats, and when emergency services were finally able to get to the scene, he would realize he lived to see the consequences of mages in a society that misunderstood them and had them gravely outnumbered.

Police and EMTs arrived first. Vern was fished from the river when the firetruck came, then warmed and questioned. Surprised at his new talent, the police recorded his statement and seemed to believe the unbelievable story.

Laz watched curiously, listened from the merman's sobering mind until he felt the bridge tremble at the arrival of an armored van. He had never seen one before, but the unit that came out of it shoved through, spoke quickly and briefly, flashing credentials that silenced the officers on the scene. "B.R.A.D" their vests read. They were sent in response to Vern's threats. Once it was discovered that he transmuted, the police were out of their jurisdiction.

The uniformed officers were put on crowed control by the superior officials and Vern was removed from the scene. Laz knew Vern had no one to call and considered briefly telling the mysterious officials the man was only a man when he made the threat, but he would have to out himself as empowered and risk being taken along with him. Although certain they would never capture him as easily as they got Vern, he did not know who he was up against nor how many innocent people would have to die for him to stay free.

'Oh well,' Laz thought. Thankful for the address he helped himself to from the merman's mind. He expected he would have Vern's place while he rested up in a hospital on a seventy-two-hour psychiatric hold, but now it seemed Laz would have the place indefinitely as Vern dealt with his felony verbal assault charge issued by the mysterious unit who took him away.

By Bread Alone

Friday:

Making a mage out of an ordinary human hit the spot, it filled a void in Laz that he once thought only opioids could. Far more satisfying than puppeteering the dead. Laz needed almost an entire day of sleep to recover and more food than the man's tiny kitchen had to offer.

When he finally rose, he called an old connect and promised double the money if he could bring him a couple of burgers and fries along with whatever he could provide for him to chase the high with. Funny thing, the fix did not last as long outside of the magical paradise as it did inside. Laz still had not recovered enough to get groceries let alone go out corpse collecting.

While he waited for his delivery, he sat to eat a bowl of cereal and water. It gave him just enough strength to peruse conspiracies online while listening to the local news. With what he had seen, he could believe anything, but he learned last year the news does not know or does not tell even half the story. They *were,* however, keeping him updated on the merman. The anchorman confirmed that Vern would be sentenced sooner than expected, thanks to the national interest his story was attracting overnight. He, like other known mages who could be pinned with a crime, were made an example of, accompanied by men in black once in custody.

Another hour passed, maybe two, Laz dozed and the knock on the door woke him up again.

"Waddup man?"

"What's up?" Q entered Laz's new place and just like old times, did not bother asking about it, knowing he may never see Laz in it again.

"I got something good for you." Q handed him his bag of greasy takeout and dropped his backpack on the once valuable sofa that now displayed a lifetime of use, "I ain't heard from you in a minute. Thought you was hit, man."

Laz could not explain the year he had so easily, so he sighed and replied, "Yeah man, I been gone, just keeping a low profile, you know."

"I feel you. Take a look around," he gestured to his pack of felonious merchandise, "I got everything."

"Just give me a half of your best green. Dealer's choice."

"That's it? You okay?" Q questioned.

"Yeah. I have been clean a while now." Laz said uncomfortable.

"Oh man, that's cool. That's cool. I only fuck with herb too. I just sell the rest of this shit to get by. I plan to finish school debt-free."

"Smart."

"Hell yeah. And my girl pregnant now too." Q said with a smile plastered on his face and a joy in his eyes.

"Wow man, congrats."

"Thanks. I'm trying to get us a spot, stop renting. You got kids?"

"Naw, not yet." Laz trusted this dude, with his money and drugs, but he had not yet told anyone of the son that the prophetess foresaw.

"Seems like it's as expensive as they say, but my plan is still the same: Make this money, don't let it make me, you know, So I sell *everything* now, man."

Laz laughed.

"I'm for real! I'll do your round up too!" He handed Laz a half-ounce of grass.

"Word? I been looking to get fresh. Meeting up with my ex soon. I can't be looking any kind of way."

Laz paid him handsomely for his order plus more than double for the food and threw in a little extra for his lady and the baby on the way. Q used to fight him on the extra he had given, but Laz assured him he deserved it more than him or the people he took or bartered it from. Q did not need to know more. He was used to characters like Laz and worse. Now Q did not even bother to count the bundle which he knew was too much. All the better, as he had gotten emotional over it in the past. Neither of them wanted a repeat.

"My setup is in the car. I'd hook you up now, but I got to meet a new client soon, first impressions are everything. I better head out in a minute, but I can come back through in a couple of hours if you'll be here."

"Yeah, let's do that. You got time to smoke?"

"Oh yeah, I got a spliff rolled up." He sat down and pulled a plastic sleeve from his pack. "I'm glad you are cleaning up now though. Shit getting too thirsty, man." He said a moment later speaking through a mouthful of smoke.

"Yeah?"

"Hell yeah, I just started selling Drops. That shit goes for twenty dollars a pill."

"Selling what?"

"Drops. You know, Re-re."

"Rezestra?" Laz asked in disbelief.

"Yup. Got someone wanting sixteen sheets. That's four hundred and forty-eight pills. She'll be good for the year... And I'll be good for a semester."

Laz noted the smug expression on Q's face and smiled for a second. Q was never smug. "I thought they stopped making that." He said suddenly more serious.

"No, it's only illegal to the public. Some private facilities can legally buy, study, test it, so they keep making it. And as long as it keeps making money on the streets, there will always be someone to steal it."

They passed the cigar of tobacco and marijuana back and forth and Laz realized how much he missed the nicotine teasing at his fiending mind. He forgot for a second that his own flesh and blood still benefited from the production of a determined mind-control substance that he believed should have been completely outlawed.

Q ground the roach into the ashtray and hopped to his feet, "Anyway. Money calls, I'll see you in a little bit."

□

It felt like a setup, but Q could not figure out a better way. He knew he was not bringing this woman or any other client to his house. He kept the house clean, so he settled for the parking lot of the busiest mall with the least surveillance to meet with some random student's mom's friend. A lot of his clients were random students. He could understand her not trusting anyone with this grand order, but this was too hot.

He was careful with the ones who bought Rezestra, don't stay long, don't take any drinks, and don't get friendly. At first, he thought it was even a clever idea to meet her on neutral territory. But now it just felt like he had set himself up for a sting, but if it were not, it could get him ahead for once. Way ahead. He waited briefly in a parking lot before the convertible pulled up.

Other than the privilege that accompanied her white skin, she seemed harmless. Maybe a little obvious in her expensive ride and too-tight red dress. If a cop car rolled by it would not be difficult to grab their attention. She slowly strolled over, calm and collected. Q glanced at his watch impatiently.

"Hey cutie," she said excitedly.

"How you doin' ma'am," he grumbled.

"Miss, please. In fact, *you* can call me Rita."

He enunciated, "How are you, Miss Rita?"

She laughed. "I appreciate you being able to fill such a big order so fast. Shame they made it illegal. It has been working miracles for me, I would hate to run out. Might turn back into a pumpkin."

"Just make sure you take one a day or every other day is better, so you can make sure you're still all there."

"You sound like a pharmacist. You're probably right. I used to think a little forgetfulness was a small price to pay for turning back the clock on my looks, but... then my neighbor gave away her car to the first kind stranger who'd asked for a ride and I just..." she put her hand on his shoulder. He cringed away, Q was only that comfortable with his wife and mother. She leaned into him.

"...Every other day," he repeated slinking away into his pack. He opened a sealed black plastic bag that would be hers and handed her a single sheet from the order. He zipped his pack ready to make a run for it if he had to.

Amused at his polite rejection, she said, "You're such a sweet man. It doesn't help you to tell me to take them infrequently. I won't need any more for a while. *Unless*..."

His head shot up, her unfinished sentence hanging over him like a threatening dagger. "Unless what?"

"Well, there is this club I went to recently, Siren. I'm in love with it. The music is good, the name is clever. Too bad they're my competition. I just have to have it. And it feels so good to get everything I want again. Supposed to be hard to get close to the owner if you don't know him. I heard from a little birdie you know him though. Perhaps you could introduce me?"

"Nah. I can't help you." Q was itching to leave.

"You don't know him?" Her bottom lip pushed out in a pout.

"I got to go ma'am."

"Miss!" she yelled correcting him again. Then she sighed, "Rita."

"You want to do business or not?" A poker face hid his desperation.

"I do. Much bigger business though. There would be a lot of consistent money in it." She said in her best persuasive voice.

"Starting to think you intend to use this Rezestra for more than just your eye bags."

"Now you don't have to be rude, I was planning on keeping you, adding you to the payroll..." She undressed him with her eyes. "Mmm, and I still might. I don't need Rezestra to make that happen." She grabbed Q's hands with hers, his backpack hit the cement as she purred in his ear, "It just comes with a lot fewer side effects than what I've just done to you, sweet pea."

He fought for a moment too big to lose in a physical match, but already transfixed by the spell spilling over his body. In mere seconds, he tensed, relaxed, and surrendered to the soporific daze.

She took his pack and retrieved the rest of her order while he was frozen in place, "See you tonight, you'll know where to be." She groped at the front of his pants and both her eyebrows shot up, "Oh yeah."

Everything blurred, shapes doubled and tripled. The parking lot rocked under his feet as he moved backward to press his back further into the side of his car, as if it would stop the world from spinning. He was nauseous and she was long gone with her order, not leaving him a dime.

Numb all over his body except for the soles of his feet, he could not chase her, but she was in his head. Her voice grew louder and louder until it engulfed his mind entirely. He listened to her seductively promising him more than she owed, hypnotizing his thoughts to match her desires and taking information to suit her needs. She knew all he knew about the owner of the club, Angel. If she could get close to him, Siren was as good as theirs.

Rita was undecided as she evaluated Angel's worth to her. Q was just a treat, but she hoped along with Siren, the owner might be another reward.

Q had tried and failed to block thoughts of Angel from his mind, protecting him at all costs. She questioned his resistance.

'You think so highly of him, but will you think the same way when you replace him tonight?' She was promising him the club, women, money, and sex. Everything, he realized, but his freedom.

Finally, the dizziness won out, he hit the pavement. After a time, he made it inch by inch to the driver's seat of his SUV, and at least now he could see straight enough to know another half-hour passed. He was at last able to drive, but her presence was still there, sending him thoughts of her pleasing herself, pleasing him. He was disgusted with himself, wrestling with trying to make the images stop, but his body was also becoming hers.

He found himself not wanting to fight but simply trying to do right by the life he had known this morning. In that same sentiment, he drove back to where Laz was, intending to tell him what happened, though not believing anyone could know what to do to reverse it.

☐

He drove up to the place Laz stayed banging on the door.

Laz would have ignored it since he was the intruder, but the noise would only have brought more attention. He swung the door open furious until he saw Q.

"What's up, man?" He asked him an octave too high.

"Let's get this over with." He pushed in with a new bag identical to his drug pack on the outside, inside it was full of varying clippers, combs, scissors, and other accessories of a seasoned barber.

"Whoa man, what happened?" Laz asked.

Q attempted to form Rita's name or speak the events that followed, but he couldn't produce the words, or ask his ally for help. He sighed defeated. "Nothing," He lied instead, "Just ain't got all day. We doin' this or what?"

Normally, Laz would have squared up to that kind of talk, but this was Q, or rather it was not. Laz fought with magic now anyhow. He sat, scoped his old friends' minds for the first time,

21

unable to get very deep in his sober thoughts. There were short passing thoughts from Q's inner monologuing, but Laz noticed he was not the only invader.

Something else he had never experienced was present and creating gaps in the little he should have been able to pick up on. Laz perceived these somethings as spores or dust or *'mites?'* he subvocalized. In response, as if they were aware of him, the tiny gap-creators formed a telepathic current that charged toward his presence.

Laz reverberated back into his wholeness when Q spoke aloud. "Spark that blunt, man." The deep timbre over his shoulder reminded him where real life was. "I'm starting to get a headache."

Laz realized he had caused them both a headache and backed off unable to pinpoint the origin of the pests in Q's mind. He wondered briefly if it was contagious. They passed the blunt while Q tapered the nape of his neck like the artist, he proved himself to be.

In less than a half-hour, Laz was a masterpiece. "You look good, man," Q said.

"I appreciate it. I'm meeting my old girl in a couple of hours. I might be a little on edge. I ain't seen her in a minute. Trying to think of somewhere nice to take her," he prodded knowing Q would be heading to some club, and soon. "She wants to meet at a diner, but I'm not with that." The white lie worked in his favor.

"You should come out to The Siren tonight. That's where my people will be." Q did not know why, but the club felt like it belonged to him already, and he knew Rita decided to keep the owner as she had him. Q did not want Laz near Rita or her near him but needed Laz to know what happened even if he could not say it.

"I think we'll do that. Thanks again," Laz tipped him again handsomely, forgiving the earlier strangeness, but not forgetting. For a moment, Q seemed back to his earlier self. Laz knew where Q would be tonight, and he intended to keep a close watch.

☐

Deana was being brave tonight and damn patient. She smoldered silently as her doctor lectured about safety and respecting herself, showing others how to treat her. She was right. That was why Deana could not tell her that Laz just changed the location at the last minute, something to give him even more control, something an addict would do if they were not sober. This was clearly and officially a mistake.

Not brave, *'Idiotic'* she corrected and cursed her past self.

Dr. Stevens did not have to say it. Deana understood in one night she was potentially undoing all the safety practices she had recently taken on, as well as over a year of progress. Besides tonight, besides Laz, she lived as if anyone was a potential captor. Even on the bus, she would not sit alone or with anyone who seemed like they took notice of her. Everybody noticed her.

Deana tuned her therapist out a while until she said exactly what Deana was contemplating. Even as crimes against women and children increase, one fact remains… "It's typically someone the victim knew."

As soon as Dr. Stevens offered the ride to the diner, it was obvious she wanted to see if Deana was being safe and pump more statistics into her head, giving her a healthy dose of fear. She had prefaced the offer innocently saying that her college friend was grateful for the help Deana was able to provide as an assistant in her practice.

"She can never find someone with a heart for her clientele." Deana was good and her empathetic boost made her irreplaceable, degree or not. Only a few credits shy it was hard to get an interview, but Stevens made a call. The woman cared for her. Deana could not say no to her offer now, her punishment for accepting help in the first place she figured, but Deana was scared enough without the last-minute talking to.

"Doctor Stevens..." The interruption sounded like a plea.

"...I'm sorry Deana. I just see that you've come so far, and we've gotten so close... I just... I'm sorry. I'm sure you will have fun tonight... But if I were your *friend*, I'd hope that it is just that. He doesn't deserve you."

"Thank you... really," She let the doctor drop her off at the original meeting place, an updated diner on the Canal Walk with the old town feel inside, warm, quaint, and blocks away from Siren where Laz insisted they meet.

"Here's my stop." she lied, "See you next week." She left the comfort of the heated seats for the cold busy street. Deana felt defeat that was not her own radiating from the car. She had not convinced her psych that this was a responsible adult decision either. Must have been the other and more obvious lie that a friend would pick her up if Laz gave her a sign of trouble.

'What friend,' the doctor had to think. Deana could feel disbelief welling up in the room then, but there was no audible protest. Just a kind offer to get her there safely, which she did, only for Deana to have to walk to another location with the autumn sun already settled behind the city. She was glad for the last rays of twilight and flat shoes to get her to the club.

Fallen Angel

Laz got there a bit earlier than he told Deana in a dark button-up that hugged his slim and toned frame like he knew she liked. Famously, she would make him wait, and he knew it. She was always late no matter how far in advance the plans were made. He was glad she was late tonight, counting on it even.

He gave his name at the door, but they had never heard of him. He paid the high cover charge and entered the scene spotting Q on the second level overlooking the dance floor. Q wasn't alone. A bunch of rough-looking guys surrounded by beautiful women who all wore the same odd, plastered smiles on their faces stood around him. Their eyes dazed as if their souls left them and all that was left were the shells of their bodies. Not an uncommon look of someone on a double or triple dosing of Rezestra he realized. Laz wondered what type of private facilities would fund the continuation of its production, but like his father always said, the world would have infinite buyers for the fountain of youth.

Almost one year of sobriety ended when he had taken that first puff of smoke this afternoon. The bud helped keep him off the pipe, but at this moment he was sure he needed a drink. Something about falling off the wagon made him expect a scold from the bartender, but the only shame during the exchange was from within. The bartender didn't know Laz, so he took two shots and a mint before checking in on Q.

The more Laz observed the more it appeared like Q owned the place. Him or his sugar mama, a pale middle-aged woman in a tight red dress, obviously selling something. *'I ain't mad at that.'* Laz thought when he first found them together. The woman was there by choice, so it appeared. No obvious signs she was double dosed at least. Of all the women in the VIP area, she would remember the night. Something other than the drugged dancers made Laz uneasy. It was a moment that looked so familiar to him he almost ignored it, but then he thought back.

It seemed like nothing at all when Q mentioned he only smoked herb until now when the cougar brought him something more addictive. His pleading eyes poorly masked his rage toward the woman, but it did not stop her fun time. There was no lying smile that hinted at Rezestra in Q, no apparent desire as he took his first line. Laz needed to know what other ways the woman had of making him obey, and hoped that Q could hang in there just a little longer until he could find out whatever the temptress had over possibly the only person in the world who saw Laz as a decent human being.

☐

Q had finally dragged himself to Rita's lair, she sealed his fate forcing herself onto him on Angel's old desk. The venom of her tongue violated his palate, and the intrusion of his soul left him feeling ashamed and filthy. She contaminated the spaces reserved only for his love. Q now outranked the former club owner. She had poisoned him the same as Q, both unwillingly and now irreversibly hers.

Rita gave them new orders. Angel would continue to deal with the product, including the women she fed with the counter aging capsules. She made it clear to him, without words that twice-daily dosing would keep them both vibrant and mentally absent.

27

She intended to get miles and miles from each of the women until she retired them with a low percentage of their earnings. Lastly, she assigned him to give Rezestra to any other crew she missed until she knew who else she was going to keep. The rest, she would have him terminate, uninterested in the fact that this team of his had become his family.

Angel's submission was all her doing, the Rezestra she fed him earlier was now wearing off, he could speak his own words, though not quite freely.

"What about the club?" He had much more to say, but it was all her hold would allow.

"I thought I made that clear, sugar," She smirked and spoke with a mildly southern voice and sweet lilt that paired well with a dangerous undertone, "The club is mine, as in not your problem anymore. I'll be here plenty to keep my eye on it. Q is gonna help me when I'm not. If I'm not here, you and everyone else will report to him. Got it?"

He knew the answer before he asked the question. The ones she took were all tuned in to her transmission. He wanted it to be a lie, a nightmare that could end. Q ran work for Angel for years, and demonic sex possession or not, he wanted to kill him for this betrayal. Though, the reasonable part of him also knew, same as him, neither of them could stop her. Neither of them could speak against what was happening inside their minds. Whatever he wanted to say as he walked by him, he could not. So, he scowled and said nothing as he walked by following the compulsion that accompanied her given orders.

Even if Q could speak up, he could not see how anyone would not just believe he was enjoying himself. Who would sympathize with him having gotten Angel's club in exchange for a little product and a stiff fuck?

Q and the vile woman walked off to sit near the railing. "What do you want with me?" he asked her, when only the two were close enough to hear one another over the music.

"Everything, baby. The world is our oyster. You're mine, and I get to be young again. I get to do it all better now."

"Why do you want *me*?"

"Have you seen yourself? A big, strong, young man like you? Total keeper." She took a shot and swayed to the music.

"That's it? You like Angel too though." She grabbed him by the collar grazing his skin and he was stunned again. She normally preferred the men quiet but humored this one. An understanding came upon him, and he began to comprehend her twisted but genuine favor of him.

"You see, I've been you and him briefly. I got just a glimpse of your character. Angel's okay, but I did steal his club. I can't really trust him. I can trust you for now. Not that either of you could cross me yet. I know eventually you're gonna turn completely, but you started nice enough, so I hope it makes you just right for me in the end." She smiled sweetly imagining.

Q could feel she was telling the truth. He wondered if she even could lie to him and then realized she would never have a reason to.

"No more questions. You wouldn't want to bore me already, would you? Live a little!" She rose pulling him and made him dance with her, "By the way, you'll forget your girlfriend soon enough,"

29

She kissed him, and he tasted it again, the bitter poison of her saliva and then the heavenly customized pheromones just for him. He could not fight, but he stopped hoping he could for a moment while the bitterness was masked. It would not last long, but he would get used to that too.

The woman he called Rita gave him the tray of even powdery lines and the metal straw. His desire to fight came back. She said nothing, but the order came to him still and his heart raced as if in preparation for work to come. She could make him obey, but she could not make him less terrified. This one sin easily avoided by his lifelong healthy fear he could become like the saddest of those whom he, his late father, late uncle, and late brother before him, served every day for decades. The cycle was supposed to end with him. He could not let it get to his son.

In his mind he resisted, but there was nothing he could do to make his body his again. All he could do was watch until he followed through on Rita's wish. First, he felt invincible and screamed out in euphoria. Short moments later, a sting came crashing down. Cursing he buckled under the intense feeling. Rita cackled until he stopped wincing and pulled himself onto a seat. He soothed himself as she caught her breath. A young woman on a Rezestra high came over to tell him that someone asked for him at the VIP entrance.

Not wanting to face anyone just yet, he just looked at the young woman, paranoid by her wide clown smile. She could not read the begging on his face to be left alone, but Rita could as easily as if the two shared in some toxic codependent synchronization.

"I got you, baby," Rita encouraged, "Trust what's happening to you cause it ain't gonna stop. But you'll never face anything alone again. I can promise you that."

He comprehended her meaning as he stood. She was not forcing him exactly, but her wanting him to get up and go made it easy for him to do. He was her servant. He got up and descended the stairs separating him from the general population of club-goers. He saw Laz. First, he was relieved to see his friend, then worried. He was not exactly, nor only his self and there was a warring of his changing minds.

He intended to ask Laz to look after his lady and kid since he could not go back to that life. Rita might let him go home from time to time, maybe even this night, but he would never really be home again. He felt unable to explain the why. A few steps to go he started fixing his mouth to at very least drive Laz away from Rita and what she might do to him if he got close enough to her. Before the words touched his lips his throat tightened to a choke to punish any sentiments formed against his master.

As he got closer to Laz, Q noticed a scent he never noticed before, like a pungent repellent, warning Q that Laz was an enemy. Q felt the speech he had thought up changing into a product of his new mind. Rita had to be protected. Unfortunately, now she was his only ally. Her and her other minions.

☐

Laz helped himself as a passenger to Q's high and was surprised to find that not only was Q not enjoying it, but the once spore-like visitors had grown noticeably to the size of needles. Laz pieced his soul back together intending to check on the guy rather than tempt the needles to charge as the spores had.

He went over to the guard at the bottom of the stairs to the VIP area, playing it cool. Laz scanned the unsmiling and hulking

31

bouncer. He noted that the needles that infected Q occupied this man too.

Again, he was not on the list, but he had been charming and explained he was an invited guest. He did not dare add magical persuasion. His words meant nothing to the guard, but his money was almost as convincing as magic. Laz generously tipped the man and waited.

Moments later, Q was in view at the top of the stairs looking glad to see Laz for a moment. Relieved, and then suddenly not. From his expression alone, Laz could see that he was not wanted here. Q's greeting proved it.

"What, nigga?"

Laz ignored the fighting words again. Swallowed his surprise and rage. This version of Q was intoxicated by magic and more. Never mind that they were on his turf surrounded by his security. They would all be in danger if Laz lost his temper.

"Yo, my bad. you said your people were hanging out. I thought maybe me, and my girl were good too." Laz tried with a smile.

"Yeah, my people and I *are* hanging out up there. Not you."

"You invited me, so I figured –"

"–You here ain't you?"

"Alright, man," he let it go, repeatedly thinking to himself, *'this isn't Q, this isn't Q,'* before he decided to strangle him with his bare hands for sport, "No problem." Still, he was sure he could not let him out of his sight.

Anyone up there was only visible if they wanted to be. Q and his old woman did not want to be seen much after this odd exchange.

Laz sent drinks over to the table with the best view of the VIP floor. The couple who occupied it thanked him. He was able to persuade them into accepting the drinks even in these times, but it took three rounds of top-shelf tequila to get them to give up their seats. From there he would only need to wait for Deana and watch the upstairs as best he could.

When she walked in, he stood, feeling suddenly awkward like only she could make him feel, but she did not notice him right away. *'Look at me'* he compelled to her sober mind, and she scrunched her lip. *'NOTICE ME!'* he insisted with all his will.

She did. Some part of her wanted to. Not enough for her to smile when she finally saw him, but enough for him. His grin did not waver.

Keep Your Tongue from Evil

Her eyes were magnets for him. She shuddered. He sat looking virtuous, handsome as ever, with his notoriously devilish smile. She hoped time would have diminished his appeal as she paced herself through the entranced crowd. He smiled and all at once her heart stopped as if it had forgotten to beat. Rekindled lust of course but accompanied by old rage and adrenaline from remembered panic attacks once confused with love.

Time slowed. Mental images rushed over her; images from violent yelling and shoving to passionate and sweating bodies in heat, and then again to unevenly matched physical combats. Her body trembled with desire and fear recollecting the chaos of their turbulent highs and lows. Parts of her still wanted his blood and too late she realized she faced the scariest version of Laz tonight: the one that could charm her into short-term memory loss, use her want for him against her. She took a deep breath and braced herself for the whirlwind of emotions that would inevitably follow him into her life.

He stood waiting at the table as she walked through a crowd that seemed to part for her.

Laz couldn't keep his eyes off her, she was stunning, "You look... ...like you've lost some weight."

Unsurprised by his insensitive statement, she climbed onto the stool beside him, "Hi to you too!"

"I'm sorry, I just mean you look great. You always did, but...

you look healthier."

"Getting clean will do that for you."

"Of course." He sat uncomfortably.

"How long have *you* been clean?" She asked in unmasked disbelief.

"About eight months." *'Until today,'* he added mentally.

Deana could not help thinking again that Laz looked so fine. She instead staved the thought off with a negative one. *'The devil is a sharp dresser too,'* she thought. Aloud she prodded, "Care to share what made you sober up?"

"Do you?" He asked, willing to bet that she would not.

"...I haven't even told my therapist that yet."

He laughed. "Thanks for meeting me." They both felt a tinge of confidence return to him.

"You should know, I have no intentions of getting close to you. And I'm not getting back with you."

"I figured. But still," he looked at her with the eyes of someone who knew what all of her felt like. "Whatever it is you wanted, I'm at your command."

Frenzied. That's what she called the feeling within herself when he looked at her like that. She tried not to smile. The emotions changed at their little table, and thanks to their differing displays, she could just barely make out who felt what. The passion was mutual, but hers immediately stifled by vining fear and wrath. His was fast blooming and overshadowed her own. Emotionally and physically, she pulled back for now, but a slip like that could get her killed. It almost had once before. Though he did not seem like the version of himself that could hurt her tonight, she would not delude herself into thinking that part was gone.

The woman in red came back into Laz's view just above Deana's head as she began to speak again. She started hesitantly, "When you're high like you were all the time, you miss things. Moments you can never get back, moments that if you were sober for, you'd never let yourself forget."

"I understand." He was divided but managing.

"Do you, Laz? I don't feel like you can even understand the half. We were completely reckless! You got me into a lot of awful habits... I'm not saying that you're to blame. I'm grown, I respect that it was my job to turn certain things down...."

Laz pretended to listen, watching the woman above, grinding on men who were each infected with the seemingly sentient spores. They all had foul plans for the night, Q too as far as he could tell. Plans or orders. It was not clear from his perspective, but from where Laz sat, Q was just as bad as the woman in red seemed to be.

She took a line for everyone she offered even to women dosed and re-dosed with Rezestra already. He had seen her throwback more shots than the entire VIP combined. Somehow, she was still vertical and to him, impenetrable. Laz attempted to probe her mind, but he was repelled. An impossible phenomenon that made Laz try repeatedly. Each time he felt his energy approaching hers, there was hate between them like natural enemies.

He used Q for lurking, but his polluted mind was full of unexpected blind spots. Things Q could observe that Laz could not. Not much could be gathered from him. Laz got a better perspective from the beautiful dancing ladies. For once in his lifetime, a reason to be grateful for Rezestra. It gave him willing victims, easy as the dead to move, but Laz had to let them continue with the previously given orders they were all following. Simple enough to execute even though they would surely forget, entertain, fuck for money, bring earnings to Red, as some of them knew her, re-dose, and repeat.

Red was their preternatural pimp. It was not her real name, but that is what most knew her as, one of many names she had given. She did not want them to know her long, but long enough that she would not only be using Rezestra on them to keep them obedient but also for its original intent, to keep them looking fresher longer.

It became necessary to infiltrate the woman's being. He wondered if she were at all human. The only familiarity beneath her outer surface was a solid mass that seemed related to the needles and spores inside the minds of many of what Laz now considered Red's harem. He did not dare toy with the angry and vibrating sphere, he did not wish to attract its attention.

He hoped Q could be emptied of Red's influence. He wanted to save him if it was not too late. Laz decided that he could not let him or any of them continue living as they were. He was not above killing Red to undo her hex, but he would need to get her somewhere more private. '*Easy*.' Or so he thought before remembering the important once-in-a-lifetime date he was currently on.

Deana's voice flowed back to him, "I shouldn't have even been *drinking* around you back then. I guess we don't have to worry about that anymore… but that's another thing, why would we come to a club when we're both clean? I'm sure as hell not dancing with you if that's what you were thinking. Are you listening?"

"Yes," he answered looking well above her.

She went on, "I know you said you stopped using, and that you want to try to make up for all the abuse, but you never can make up for the type of damage you've caused me." He squinted his eyes, she assumed in concentration and confusion. His consciousness was whole, but his attention unfocused.

"You know I don't care about your intentions for having me come here because this is about what I need. If you can't give me that, then there is nothing that we have to talk about."

It appeared Red noticed him now, noticed Deana. Everyone noticed Deana. Always. It was his more than once excuse to punish her, but he had buried that version of himself along with his mother. He had sworn it to himself that that part was gone, or risk becoming the monster his father called him.

"I'll do anything," he said before slipping his attention to the floor above again.

After too long of Red's stares, making Laz beyond uncomfortable, he attempted to suggest she find another person to poison. He had more than enough will to inflict the warning and prayed her massive blockage was subdued by the thousands of dollars' worth of drugs she had done. Yet again to simply enter the woman was like dancing around a hot mine. Her energy felt like emptiness orbiting around a searing orb of metallic threats. It dared him to speak. Her preying stares at Deana dared him not to.

A simple thought transmitted from Laz's mind, *'She's taken!'* and the mass bit back with a voltaic declaration that shocked Laz's mind and soul sending him back to a telepathically tased body.

Deana stopped speaking for a moment, terrified of the changing feelings she noticed. A shift from assured confidence that she suspected was a product of Laz's ego, to a damning fear of inadequacy. She tried to ignore his energies and speak through it, but suddenly, there was intense pain and she had weakened along with him. Deana detached herself from his feelings instinctively, willing for the moment to trade in her new power altogether.

Even twisted up, his face, to her, was pleasant. She felt an overwhelming need to coddle him before the relief of repulsion that followed as she severed her emotional strings from him.

"Are you alright?" she asked, trying to be civil. When he did not answer, she leaned closer to peer into his glazing eyes and smelled mint poorly masking a heavy smell of brown liquor. Laz used to love a dark and sultry drink with dinner. He used to say it was a sign he was a man of luxury. She was disappointed to see that he still was.

He screamed internally before his body could join in and then aloud as he became one entity, "AAAAH!" He fell backwards toppling off of the stool and onto the hardwood floor.

"What is wrong with you?" Deana yelled from above him, but the question lacked concern. She continued, "You lied. You're high, aren't you?" She waited for an answer, but he said nothing. Full of apparent fury toward him, but more with herself for even trying, she began to storm off.

The damage shocked him so badly he could not speak

coherently or even think for a moment too long for Deana. He was not clean. Not anymore. So, he let her leave. He watched her steps until he could not see them from where he lay on his back, and then moved his head stiffly to look up at the second floor again.

The woman he could not truly enter was a real mage. During his party-stopping fall, she made for a door at the bottom of the staircase and behind the guard. All eyes on Laz, he laid there silenced physically, but managed to tail her repellent energy with his as best he could until the stink was yards away from the building.

He let her go too, if for no other reason than to conserve any power that remained after the devastating blow. It took a lot of extra power to hold on tightly to what resisted him. For now, his broken heart and wounded spirit would both remain unsatisfied.

This was as near to fatality as he had been in a while, but Laz did not fear for his life. Tonight, was about saving Q who had finally made himself visible to the first floor again. They looked knowingly to one another. Q shook his head and vanished into shadows again, embarrassed at his invitee.

☐

Siren spat Deana back out onto the cracked pavement. The lullaby of entrancing tunes cut off as the door shut behind her. It had not seemed so loud inside, but she couldn't hear anything on the street. She clutched her jacket around her hoping for comfort to traverse the sea of strange faces. She looked at the long stretch of sidewalk between here and her apartment building, and back to the club entrance. Feeling caught between a rock and a hard place, she chose to continue, desperate for home.

She went on cursing her bad choices and the state of a world so dangerous that there were now so few ways to get home safely when you had no one. She gave a moment's consideration to taking chances with a rideshare app, with the hope of not ending up with a sketchy driver. Too many Rezestra victims get taken that way. She walked on. Head held high but shivering a little.

The chatter around her swirled, and she could not make out a single word. The wailing of police cars warned of their approach, but she could not pinpoint the direction from which they came. She could feel the coming panic attack and tried looking for anything visually pleasing to help her relax.

She turned her attention to neon lights that still flickered "Welcome" along the strip despite the thick tension and mistrust of the current climate. Each bar had the same memo, with cover charges at record highs and the drinks cheap since no one was buying. Another effortless way to be made a victim these days, yet people still wanted to be around people and enough of them felt invincible. Some probably were.

Deana began to feel herself blending into the crowd. Sounds began to clear up and her heart calmed. Just as she thought herself clear from panic, she was met with a blast of fire inches from her face. She gasped inhaling smoke, coughing.

"Hey, hot stuff!" A magically enhanced creep shouted after the snap of blinding flame died down. Deana stumbled and ran around to get some space away from the pyro.

"Don't be scared!" He called after her cackling, "Let me light your fire baby!"

She kept going, pushing past other pedestrians, and slammed

41

right into a ghost of her past. Familiar arms caught her just before she hit the ground. They stood her upright.

"Parker," she said breathlessly.

They were a sort-of-ex with whom she was still technically on good terms with but ghosted after their brief affair. They finally let it go and stopped bothering her online. Unlike Laz, they could take the hint.

By chance they stepped into her path, trying to see why a man was yelling and why a woman was running, but they did not expect her.

"Deana? Wow! Quelle surprise!" they greeted in French beginning to smile. The faint rasp of their voice brought overwhelming relief. She held to Parker's natural calm as if it were an old habit. Something she never noticed doing when the two briefly dated, but she let it soothe her without question now. She could feel their presence more precisely than anyone else's on the entire bustling sidewalk. The panic attack faded even though something in Parker made her think she was not exactly safe.

Parker glanced at the pyro still lingering and Deana could feel them instantly change from enamored to protective.

"You out here alone?" They asked Deana still glaring daggers over her head at the laughing man.

"Yeah."

"Not anymore. You can stay with us." They gestured to their friends. Four other women or non-binary individuals, all attractive. Nothing less was expected of Parker's entourage. Instantly she

42

remembered why they did not last, but at least she could get home all right.

"Do you think your friends could give me a ride home?"

"We barely fit in the car as it is... and I think they want to keep chilling..."

"Oh. Right." Deana said.

"... But I can walk you home."

"Really? No... no, you have fun."

"Of course, I will! I'm not leaving you alone out here." They turned to their friends, who stood smoking up against cement walls, "I'll catch up with y'all later."

The pair began to head off in the direction Deana was running. Parker pretended they were joking when they suggested staying vigilant and holding hands. Deana could feel that they too were terrified, and an old flame Deana thought was out stirred within them. It reminded her to be careful not to get home too quickly with Parker.

Deana was prepared to say no to a hot night with Laz, the danger being so obvious, but Parker had their own brand of torment. If she let them in, they would make her feel like she was the only important thing for the moment, but heaven only knew how quickly Parker could find a new interest. Their one deal-breaking flaw. Tonight, Deana was safe, but tomorrow if she were not careful, there could still be heartbreak.

"I always hoped I'd run into you around here," they started, "but then again, I also kinda hoped you moved somewhere safer."

"Yeah, the few blocks home feel like miles suddenly."

"What were you doing out here alone, Dea?"

She breathed, hesitated, *'Being a grown-ass woman. You sound just like the cops, the president, every man in America right now, and half the women. Why is it that I have to stay home and imprison myself because motherfuckers don't know how to act?'* She ranted internally.

"That wasn't exactly my plan." Deana offered aloud, "I had someone drop me off near Siren."

"Oh, and who was supposed to take you home?" Deana heard the underlying accusation, she felt in them the envy that toiled with the confused upset.

"I was meeting Laz." The truth was not better, but unlike Parker, it was consistent.

"Dea..."

She could almost taste the sourness of Parker's disappointment. "we're not together..." she started.

"I'm saying, when I met you, I thought you'd never want to see him again."

"Yeah, me too... It doesn't even matter now because he lied to me before I even showed up. He said he stopped using, but he was drinking and *had* to be on pills or something because he nodded off at the bar *as* I was talking to him. It was only a second, but I got out of there. I don't want *anything* to do with him *ever* again. I just thought...." she laughed at herself and continued "I just thought I'd get some."

"Some...? ...oh, please tell me you were about to say closure."

"No, I think I got that."

"So why would you let him..."

"It's been a while, okay! I left alone, didn't I? I couldn't let him know where I live... I don't know what I was thinking. He said he changed, I had to see for myself, I guess."

"But how did he find you?"

"I found him..." She continued before Parker vocalized their judgment. "I know. Stupid, but I had good reason. Some things I needed to come clean about. For my own sake, you know?"

"Did you?"

"No, and I may never, but I had to at least try. It would be so much easier if I could. My karma would certainly be better for it."

"Feel like talking about it now?"

'Yes.' She said internally, but aloud she answered, "Not really."

Parker, like the gentle soul they could be, changed the subject. Seamlessly the pair slid back into old chemistry. "You still watching the news like an old lady?" They asked her.

"I just can't look away! Every time I think that the world is done bringing to light some crazy three ring circus of a story, cut-to commercial and they're back with more!"

They chuckled. "Yeah, I can't even watch anymore. At all. I'd rather not know at this point. It's too much."

"What does your grandma have to say about all of it? I know she's probably having a field day with the 'I told you so's.'"

Parker's natural calm turned to ice, and they began to silently mourn. Deana didn't want to believe what they were feeling but it was clear.

"She died." They looked away.

"Oh, God. I'm so sorry, Park. How..." she choked, "When did this happen?"

"About three months ago."

"Months? And you didn't tell me? Have you been dealing with this all on your own?"

"I tried to call you." They peeked at her in their peripheral to see that she understood.

"Oh." Deana's heart dropped as she remembered her not answering their calls as petty revenge for their neglect.

"It doesn't matter, I'm fine." It did not take an empathic boost to know that was a lie. Their grandmother was almost a parent to them. Deana remembered how big of a deal it was, to everyone who knew, for her and Parker's gran to meet.

It was only once, and they bonded over their shared love of trashy media outlets. The vibrant septuagenarian yelled for Deana to take it as a compliment when Parker began to rush her out of the house. She had just told Parker that Deana was a keeper, and it was a clear enough sign that they agreed with her. The relationship fell apart too shortly after that.

"My cousin Monica moved into the house, and she's been taking care of most of everything," Parker said.

"You mean you didn't get the house? You did everything for your grandmother. I could see if she left it to your mom. Maybe even your aunt, but your *cousin*? The one from *Cali*? The one that comes to town *once* every two *years* or something?"

"I always knew Monica was her favorite. Those two were always on the phone. Guess that outweighs the 3-plus days a week I was with her for the last 11 years."

"Well did she leave you anything?" Deana asked.

"Books."

"Books?"

"Yeah... she left me some old books."

"Oh! You love old books!"

"Yeah... I do... Because she loved them, wouldn't let me touch them until recently, and I could tell Monica is jealous that I got them, but I practically grew up in that house. I just thought it'd be mine."

"What did you do with them? The books."

"I told Mo just keep them in the attic for now. I was thinking of selling them. they're old as dust and they gotta be worth thousands each."

"You would sell your Gran's precious books?"

"You sound like Monica."

"Then we're probably right."

"I figured. That's why I told her to keep them where they are for now. I guess I couldn't actually sell them, but they just reminded me of how I ignored her when she talked about magic and potions and charms for years. Now people are getting surges of power left and right, and she dies? Right as I finally started to see it. How can I ever forgive myself? I don't deserve her precious books."

Parker was still in denial, still angry and bargaining. Deana knew the stages of grief well. Parker had not mourned enough. She let them go on venting.

"I think that's what the books are for. Maybe she knew she wouldn't live to see me believe. She'd been trying to get me to my whole life. My dad said she was just a funny old lady. To humor her if I wanted but leave it at the door, and mom never got involved. She probably knew too, but... I just knew I didn't want anything to do with it, and now I'm thinking I missed out on a chance to know an important part of my grandmother's beliefs."

"Keep the books... keep them at the house. See what's in them. Get to know her that way. Monica and your grandmother too."

"You're probably right. Mo's really into the witchy stuff. She and gran talked about it all the time."

"Maybe you two will get along well." Deana was hopeful for them, that the loss might instigate a new bond.

"Maybe. She and I were close as kids before she moved away."

"So, Monica knows a lot about magic, huh? Maybe she can teach us how to discover powers within ourselves." Deana said optimistically.

"Maybe. She always believed. We played witches as kids, but she never let it go, and apparently, she was right not to. Who would have guessed that? She'll be a fine teacher or whatever my gran had planned for us."

"So, does she have power?"

"You should ask her yourself some time," Their smile was cut short again. As if something buzzed by, they swatted their ear and looked over their shoulder.

"What's wrong with your ear?"

"What? Oh, I thought I felt something... it's nothing, but ... let's walk a little faster."

"Wait, what's wrong?"

They sighed. "A guy a little way behind us... he's staring pretty intensely. I don't know I think... It's just a weird vibe."

"So, what you have powers now?"

Parker looked at Deana sarcastically, and they could not help but smile, laugh. Then they peered back at the man. He began heading the opposite way. The feeling stopped. "Maybe I'm just being paranoid. The world is really different now."

They walked silently a moment on roaring streets, passing bars, restaurants, clubs, and hundreds of people in varying states of sobriety, but as one man approached, slow and staring, Parker felt an urge. Deana could not describe what changed, but there was bravery and fear, and confusion as Parker calculated an approaching man who did not stand out to Deana for any reason. Why he was different from the thousands of others they had already passed she could not tell, but she got a sense, barely. Nothing scary, but not enough of anything. It was as if this man were an almost empty human shell. Lights were on and no one seemed to be home.

Parker grabbed her by the arm and pulled her tight by their side. She decided to trust them. It was that, or start a fight here in the street with them. Plus, they were certain. They both remained quiet as the shell of a man passed them by. Deana did not know him, but something was a bit familiar about his vibe as he got close enough to touch. At this too close for comfort range she could get a better read. The few emotions she could pick up were raw and reptilian. He stared as he walked by and stopped to turn and continue to watch them. Parker kept looking over their shoulder as they continued moving forward. Deana looked between the man, Parker, and the direction the two of them were headed. She realized he must have been on something, '*Rezestra*,' she guessed.

"Sorry," Parker said letting go of her jacket after another few steps. Much more gently, they held her hand again, "let's just... pick up the pace, okay?"

"What was that about?" She sounded pissed, but her curiosity won the moment.

"Call it intuition. I got a bad feeling, that's all."

"I could tell... That's my power. In case you were wondering."

"What's that?" Parker still had not stopped looking back.

"I could tell you got a feeling before you reacted."

"You know me well enough. I'm sure you can tell when I'm feeling off."

"No... you weren't feeling off, you were feeling defensive... protective, territorial... And I wasn't even looking at you. Trust me, I'm watching the scene just like you are, but you noticed something weird about that guy. So did I. And I'll tell you just what if you tell me what you felt."

"You know what I felt."

"Yeah, but why? Are you an empath too you think?"

"I... I don't know Deana. We're all kind of empaths and psychics on some level, right?"

"Oh, come on! You said you believe in this stuff now. You can't exactly deny it anymore. What did you feel?"

Parker did not reply.

"Fine, I'll go first. I didn't feel much of anything. And I can feel some people more than others, but... It wasn't like I wasn't picking up on him, it was like there wasn't much to pick up on. It was weird. But it's a new power for me, like everyone I guess."

"Not everyone." Parker said plain.

"What do you mean?"

"It's just becoming news, but it's not new for everyone. My grandmother wasn't wrong, remember, about anything, but something's changed. I don't know what, but it's not good. I wish my gran was here, I bet she'd know exactly what changed. It'll be the first thing I check her books for."

It was Deana's turn to lighten the mood. "I hear some people get mental and physical powers."

"I hope my physical power is something useful, like cloning myself so one of us can take a vacation that doesn't turn into work." Said Parker dryly.

"Come on invisibility!" Deana crossed her fingers as if she were hoping to roll a hard eight. "Then a walk home could just be a walk home."

"I am still not convinced your empathy is exactly super," Parker said bursting her bubble.

"Oh, it definitely is. and now you got me thinking I may have always had it. It makes sense. Do you remember when we first started dating and we waited to sleep together?"

"How can I forget? We made it an entire three weeks." More sarcasm.

"You joke, but you're forgetting how hard it was spending hours in the gym seeing me in spandex and following me to the showers..." Deana said wanting them to remember, knowing they could not have forgotten the body they helped her create for herself.

"Oh yeah... Three w*hole* weeks." Parker exaggerated the words.

"Exactly," Deana could see them remembering, transfixed by the thought. "And then when I finally put it on you..." There was no end to the statement, but she took joy in reminding them that she got under their skin too.

"We spent a glorious week in bed." Parker was miles away.

Deana brought them harshly back to the moment. "More like a glorious three days before you got tired of me."

"What? No, I didn't!" Parker exclaimed.

Deana continued as if they hadn't spoken, "But still the sex was incredible and for those first 3 days work was a total blur. I have no clue what happened at all. No memory of any of it and no one said boo."

"So, your role is redundant, and you think you have superpowers." Parker mused.

"No! I am *vital,* thank you very much. Everything goes through my desk! *Extremely* sensitive material... and I managed to be amazing on autopilot." She bragged.

"Still not sure that means you're an empath."

"Something was guiding me. Empathy, maybe some clairsentience."

"Sure. why not." They laughed lightly. "...I'm sure I'm remembering correctly though. that was a good week. we were joined at the hip other than work."

"And then at the end of that week, you bailed on me."

"I didn't bail on you."

"Somehow I couldn't keep your interest after that."

"That's not true."

"You're right, I'll rephrase that... you had too many other interests."

"... Dea, I was just... things were getting serious so fast."

"Things were serious before the sex, Parker. You even introduced me to your gran, I was supposed to meet your parents soon after... our pace wasn't overwhelming you until we started sleeping together."

"I'm saying, I was just getting my life off the ground. I was working and traveling so much..."

"I could have gone with you or waited, but you wanted to be an international ho, right?"

"It's not like you didn't mean anything to me. I just needed that break. To focus on my work and meet people outside my world."

"Yeah, as I said, other interests."

"Dea, I still–"

"It's okay, Parker. Really. I forgave you already. And myself too finally. I just had to get that off my chest."

"Then why didn't you ever call me back?"

"Because you left the country, and slept around, and then tried to come back to me like it was nothing!"

"Because no one else mattered to me. You gave Laz another chance. Does he deserve it more than *I do*?"

"He doesn't. There are no other chances for him. I just wanted to get laid that's all."

"Well, the night is young." The smile cracked their hard face and then tension melted with it. Parker hated to be serious and much as Deana pretended not to, she appreciated it and unknowingly leaned into it.

"That's not funny," she laughed.

"I'm serious, Deana, I'm happy to hook up with you."

"Yeah, *tonight* maybe."

"Dea, –"

"You trying to tell me, you're ready to be off the market Parker?"

"I don't know. I just don't want to spend any more time with anyone else who isn't the one."

First baffled at the implication that she might be their one, and then she composed herself knowing her demons all too well. "Sounds like there is a story there," she humored. Her last defense.

They began to confess about their roommate. Better to clear that up now, "She and I were really good friends, and we should have stayed that way. Now things are weird. She was gonna move out, but she hasn't yet... I don't know, but she definitely hates me now. It's just not worth it to make such a mess of things with people who you admire. You know?"

"I know." Deana let go of their hand and the surrounding feelings became murky. Too many conflicting and blending things that she could not isolate to name. Parker could be so simple and yet suddenly far too complex.

Again, they became simple to decipher. She looked up at them in time to see them brush frantically as if waving off another buzzing fly. Something that was not a bug put them on high alert. Deana was sure they were right this time.

Touch Me and See

Laz waited, but not long. Putting first things first, he focused energetically on Q completely as he was still out of view. Anxious he gave just a few minutes to try to pick up whatever he could from their dark corner of the club. Then he would allow himself to see if Deana got off the street alright.

Red was off his radar, but heavily on his mind and adding an additional distraction in his search for information. There was already too much else to make sense of. Shielded and shocking, leaving him embarrassed and too shaken up to follow, he let her go, but he could not just let her go. Red was running the show and needed to be dealt with. He wondered why such a powerful mage would ever let him go alive after prying in her mind. *'Unless,'* he thought, *'she has an agenda.'* In her line of business, a seasoned mage would be worth a fortune to her alive.

Laz always had abilities; he just did not know they were special. Once that became known, he learned quickly to keep them secret. His private advantages were still not so safe to share. He wanted to tell Deana, but she had been on the receiving end of one of his powers too many times to confess now. A power he had renounced when he got clean, but the habit would not completely die. She could not know about any of his power, at least not yet. Especially not the one he would use to follow her tonight. His attention was divided enough though Red needed to be found, but if Q was at Siren she had to eventually come back.

One useful college graduate out alone and not being smart

proved easy to influence. The boy was stocky, dim-witted, drunk enough to control, but not so drunk he could not stand. Laz found him to be a perfect pair of eyes for a while, the combination helping him preserve energy as he strolled casually wanting to rush. A few short minutes of observation here and there was fine, but the continuous manipulation quickly began to drain him.

As if Laz had two minds, he clung tight to a drink to stay aware of his physical self, and in another, he walked. Like an intense workout, he could feel himself getting more and less powerful with each demand. He let himself be carried to her but used his strengths to stay alert in the blurred mind. He desired her and to the body, it was a command to find her. He accepted it as a rushing frat, but his mind was free enough to have its own ideas about what he would do once he found her.

'Nothing!' Laz demanded again. He stopped the thought from continuing or he would have turned the boy around to meet his end. Laz contemplated using his beating heart like a toy but spotted Deana yards ahead. Expecting to find her alone, he almost missed her. Like a mongrel, Laz grumbled, twitched, and seethed, as he was mentally prepared to dominate the slender figure that walked next to his most precious thing.

Almost as if they heard him thinking from his seat at the bar, the person walking with Deana turned to face the body Laz observed from with a mean grit. The only part of the man's face he actively controlled were the eyes and he stared back curious. His position made, and thus out of time with this body, he ordered the host back to Siren by making him think he had forgotten something.

This new vessel was much more tempting. He had disturbed something in them. He 'or... maybe she,' was courting Deana. So, he left the body as confused as a sobered-up Rezestra victim. There

58

would be time to decide what to do with him later. Even though the judge and jury let him go for "alleged" sex crimes, he had been discovered guilty by Laz, the Executioner.

He did not waste energy pulling himself back together, but instead lingered alone and semiconscious for an attractive host-partner nearby to partly possess. He head-hopped in a few briefly before Deana's escort could notice, wanting to get in their mind but worried they would notice in front of Deana. *'Maybe later,'* he thought and settled for at least getting a clear look at them.

Laz cursed wondering when and why she was so willing to leave with someone else, and what might come next. He got closer and closer behind them, followed a block and then two, and lost track of distance before deciding he needed someone walking toward them. He needed to get a good look at the person with Deana before he totally burnt out. She had her fantasies, and he had a hunch.

A passing stoner was kind enough to lend his view as he walked by the pair. Laz did not need him for anything but looking and he was already watching Deana. He thought she was lovely, as did anyone with eyes. Though he would never disrespect her date, Laz needed him to get a good look at them, size them up. The compulsion to look was there, Laz only nudged.

Just as he thought. Deana was double cuffed *with* some *'pretty-boy-looking stud,'* probably someone who had waited for him to fail tonight or there to make sure she did not leave with him, he presumed. They noticed him again then as he incensed. Probably could sense the rage he inevitably transferred to the guy. His demeanor was initially cool and in control, but Laz managed to affect his mood anyhow like a backseat driver. Just enough to harsh the high.

He left the stoner and gathered his being. He was still holding the tumbler, but it had not stopped him from forgetting his fleshly self. He was being stupid, careless, and it earned him looks from the bartender who had threatened to cut him off if he kept dozing off at the bar.

Laz was not certain he could have affected the mood of the stoner enough to change how he felt about the passing attractive couple. His thoughts were ordinary and pleasant, but Deana's real date was able to sense something off. Maybe even sense him as he was, in the bar. Assuming getting mad was somehow getting him caught, he decided to work with that, scare them off, and take none of the blame.

He needed a tool malleable to him yet already a foreboding character. The only living types out alone now were the brave, stupid, dangerous, or extremely faithful. Any among them with lowered will or inhibition were at his disposal and perfect for the assignment. He wanted to be sure they were triggered and paying attention, perhaps get a message to Deana if he could think of something, scare '*the queer*' at the very least.

He got in place ahead of them just a little bit. A wary street profit continued his sermon even as Laz slipped under the drunken hood of his consciousness, not alerting anyone, he hoped, to his presence. He watched through the windows out to the world as the homeless man saw it, burning in real-time. He believed himself righteous to suffer at these end of days as he waited, powerless and fearless for coming doom and eternal salvation. Laz let him ramble. "For with thy sorcery were all the nations deceived!"

He spat as he preached at the top of his soot-lined lungs, "Fallen, fallen is Babylon the great, and is become a habitation of devils. Come forth, my people, out of her, that ye have no fellowship with her *sins*, and that ye receive *not* of her plagues!"

Laz used the lengthy monologue to better calm himself until just the right moment when he spotted the approaching pair. They pretended not to notice the old, borrowed flesh and bones he wore as most did. Yet like anyone, they could not miss him. He would make sure they did see him when the time came to make his move.

Laz pegged Deana's company as a low-level psychic with a recent boost in ability. Helpful, but still common. He did not know if Deana had power but thought it might be funny to make the vagabond think that they both practiced magic. Like a dog to an attacker, he thought, '*sic 'em.'*

□

The cardboard sign read, "Sorcerers – their part shall be in the lake that burneth with fire and brimstone." Deana and Parker silently agreed to ignore it, but once within seven feet of the man, he zeroed in on Parker. Looking down his nose as they passed – for once, silenced in his monologue – he locked eyes with Deana to offer her a private sermon.

He yelled again, "A voice told me you were a fornicator and a sorceress!" the last word rattling in Deana's ear, "You're going to hell if you don't repent whore!" He leaped behind them and followed shouting louder, he addressed the crowd, "whores and witches we have among us folks! with the likes of nymphs like these, the city will fall!"

Deana and Parker ignored him like no one could, not slowing. The vagabond followed with only a bit of a distance. A local came out of a restaurant to break up the uncomfortable display. An old man too, but healthier, matching his volume without any violence.

"Hey, hey, hey, Henry, what I tell you about all that, huh? He shoved a steaming to-go bag into his frail torso, shooed him off. "Stay off that bottle for the night, alright?"

The street profit watched them another moment. Calculated. And suddenly he was full of only the desire to eat.

"Sorry about that. Henry is not a people person. I have never seen him that aggressive before. But I learned a long time ago that if you fill him up it'll shut him up."

"Thanks, Al" Parker said. "Deana this is the creator of the best apple pie in the world."

"Oh, why thank you! You had enough of them to know, so I am inclined to agree. Hehe, Ain't no secret, I use apples and a little bit of pear, but I got my blend of flavors that takes it over the top."

"It's the glaze I can't get enough of," Parker complimented.

"Well, that's just a simple icing," Al replied. "Come in for a slice, on the house! My wife won't let me bring home the leftovers anymore."

"Smart woman, I wasn't aware I lived this close to the best apple pie in the world. "Deana smiled. "Sometimes, ignorance is bliss. I better not take any chances having a slice."

Al laughed heartily, his belly shaking.

"We should probably get off the street anyway," said Parker, "Deana seems to be attracting the wrong types tonight," they joked.

"Must be the full moon. It was nice seeing you though, and thanks for stopping the show."

"No problem. I understand, it is crazy enough out here as it is without me keeping you later. I have been thinking of closing part-time, and I started keeping my wife and young ones home after sundown. My boy AJ and I have been taking extra hours to cover the block, you know. Like a neighborhood watch kind of thing. Can we help get you where you're going?"

"No, we're okay. I'm not too far now," Deana smiled, wishing the man were kin to her, thankful he was understanding of her new fear of the night.

"Oh, just a couple blocks, I insist. AJ! AJ!" He yelled into the restaurant. "We didn't use to take breaks during dinner, but I been trying to keep some extra staff so that some of us can assist in making others feel safe. I don't know what I can really do, but I can't do nothing. I know you don't need the help, but could you humor me, let us walk a little while with you just 'til we know you're alright?"

More help she could not refuse. "Sure," Deana said. "Power in numbers, right?" She felt no malice in either of them. Parker seemed to relax around the old chef.

He smiled; his son came out with their jackets. The four walked a couple of awkward blocks. It was not public condemnation awkward, so Parker and Deana did not complain. They humored the man as he asked about their lives and indulged in some conversation with him. His son tried not to be too embarrassed when he began to turn the conversation to the state of Deana's love life.

"Enough about us," Deana dodged, "Tell me about you, Al."

"A fixture of this neighborhood" he called himself.

"Dad!" AJ noticed his father was painfully unaware that he was intruding on a potentially romantic stroll. "Maybe we should get back to the restaurant. It's about time to start closing duties."

"Not yet. We're almost at the last bar for a few blocks. The least we can do is get them that far."

The last club on the walk was a huge place that stood alone called Mynx. A couple of floors and enough DJs to fill it all. A loose dress code meant that anyone could get in wearing almost anything or almost nothing. A trio of middle-aged smokers laughed, coughed, and joked loudly just outside. The crowd at a place like this was inevitably as diverse as the city it catered to, but everyone was eager to make new friends. They provided no additional moods far as Deana could detect.

The one woman among them, white, with a high and long black ponytail, looked flashy in her form-fitting red dress and gold jewels. She spoke inviting them into the spot. "Your night won't be complete until you check this place out. It's live." She continued to hype the place up. The two black men with her cosigned her statements with nods and 'mmhmm's.' She promised unlimited drinks on her tab.

Parker looked questioningly at Deana remembering how she used to mesmerize the room when she danced, but Deana was trying desperately to sense anything of the three. The men were dulled to her. They were having fun, but spikes of fear snuck in. She turned her focus to the woman and there was still nothing.

Al spoke in the silence to the still hopeful woman. "I think they were gonna call it a night, actually." I was just seeing them to safety before my son and I get back to work."

"Oh, well, I assure you they'd be safe with us, Mr...?"

She extended a hand to him, and he shook it. "Call me Al."

"Al, I'm Gina." She turned and shook the son's hand. "You guys should join us for a round of drinks. Maybe we can share a dance before you go on." The father and son looked at one another, then smiled at Gina.

"You boys go ahead," she continued, "Use my name at the bar, us ladies will be right in." The father and son went in and the two men that were smoking with her followed.

"I guess I could go for a dance," Parker said to the woman who then tossed the butt of her cigarette. Parker gently went for Deana's hand. "If you're up for it."

"Great!" The woman called Gina interjected. Deana still had not spoken but followed Parker and the woman up the stairs without haste, slowing Parker down. The woman held the door open for the two of them and Parker hesitated before Deana reached the top. She stopped too. Deana felt the change in them. It was the fear again more intense and sudden than the homeless man stirred up. Mistrust overwhelmed them, but Parker only looked again at Gina.

"Something wrong?" Gina asked.

"N-no." Parker lied sounding unconvincing.

Deana squeezed their hand, not moving. They looked back. There was a moment of telepathic communication between them, but Deana needed to say it, her form of therapy. "I think I would prefer to go home on second thought."

"Is it something I said?" Gina joked.

Deana was honest. "Just can't be too safe these days."

"We can't let fear stop us from living." Gina offered the street wisdom as a last attempt. "I'd be happy to drive you home afterward."

Deana squeezed Parker's hand again, and they said to Gina, "Really, if she wants to go now, I am happy to call it a night."

Deana could not feel the woman's defeat, but she portrayed it well as she spoke. "Aww, well it was nice to meet you both. You two make a lovely couple." She held her hand out again to shake the one Parker still had free. Parker reached back uncomfortably with their weaker hand. Deana watched them as they again ignored the feeling the woman brought them.

Deana's eyes widened as the hands approached one another in slow motion. She pulled. Parker almost fell into her down the cement steps and away from the woman in red. Parker bothered to wave goodnight and they sped off again.

☐

It was only cheap fun sicking the fire and brimstone street preacher on Deana and her friend. Laz let go of the homeless man when the restaurateur stepped in, never intending to cause real trouble. He hoped Deana would go home alone, but she was safe for now that was all he needed. So, he kept his concentration with his body for a time, refocusing on Q and others around him for, perhaps, too long.

The club was a convincing front for their money-over-money operation. Women were high on Rezestra and other poisons, dirty dancing between Johns. Behind closed doors, each of them purged their night's earnings surrounded by others busy making plans for dealing higher volumes of narcotics to bigger fish. The VIP lounge provided them all a place to tempt high-dollar prospects. Still, there were no signs of Red except in the pieces of her radiating in Q and a few other chosen leaders.

Laz needed to calm himself to check on Deana undetected. Another drink and then he could see her get home safely.

He found them again, and like before, they were not as he expected to find them. The man from the restaurant and another younger man now walked with them. He was relieved by the current additions. No one messed with larger groups of people unless they had the kind of abilities that made you forget to count heads. He had only just decided to abandon the host he used before noticing the woman called Red.

Just then, he wanted to run toward them in the body he controlled and rush the woman, take her down and scream for them to run, but he could not risk having any feelings at all right now. He needed them to save themselves and not be distracted by his presence. He waited readily; to run-on foot, to kill her with his magic if she touched Deana.

He watched the woman touch the older man, and then saw her touch the younger one, sure that was all it took for them to be hers. They went inside the club easily and Red honed back in on the remaining two. When they began to follow the woman up the stairs of the distant and booming building he took a step, two, three behind them, planning to follow in this current body until he could run to them in his. He would not risk losing them in this crowded space.

He began to pick up the pace. The body could not move far enough fast enough, but then Deana's date stopped just outside of the door, an arm's reach from the living succubus.

He paused in tandem, waiting a second that felt like minutes. Red reached out to touch, and no doubt infect one or both of them, he agonized, prepared to leave the man he wore in the street to get there.

But Deana smelled a rat and held her date in place. '*Good girl,'* he thought and then regretted it. Hoping Deana's date would stay in the moment. Another long second and Deana pulled them narrowly to safety.

The woman lingered a moment outside watching them leave. He watched too. They ran. Red was not faster than any ordinary human, he concluded as she stood there. They were safe again, at least for now. The desire to follow and see where she lived overcame him, but he felt eyes leering. Red made him. If for nothing but his oddly watching her prey escape. He waited for her to react. She only slinked inside, gazing on him until the club entry shut between them.

You Will Find Rest for Your Souls

The apartment building was finally in sight. Streetlamps and loud neighbors out in the late-night made Deana feel safer than they ever had. "Why do I feel like we escaped death at least once tonight?"

Parker did not say anything. Just shook their head as a wash of relief fell over them that matched hers.

They ran the three flights up and doubled over in laughs once safe on the inside of Deana's apartment. "I can't believe I almost did that walk alone!" She screamed pressing her hands into her head.

"I still can't believe you almost went home with Laz."

"I know, but if you'd ever had a dry spell, you might understand."

"Ouch! I take a break now and again, but no, not long, I guess... I do miss one thing though... being with someone I care about." Parker waited for a response standing a little closer to Deana. She tried to read them, but they had her dazed. "I made a mistake taking us for granted."

"Really?" she could feel that they meant it right now in the moment, but Parker's mind changed with the wind.

"There's a potential here. It deserves a chance."

She snapped out of it, "Don't Park..." So, Parker did not.

Instead of professing what they wondered might be love, they turned to go.

"You're going out there? Alone? *Now*? I don't think so! Have you not considered your *own* safety?"

"I probably would have noticed by the time I went back out in the dark. I could call Mo to pick me up. She'll be a little upset, but she'll understand."

"Or... you could call her tomorrow. I would love to have you here tonight. You might have sort of saved my life."

"Your roommate won't mind if I stay?" They nodded to the additional bedroom door in the familiar apartment.

"Haven't had a roommate for a while now. Please, stay." Deana kissed Parker then, and it was as if no time had passed, the bitterness for the moment evaporated as they fell back into old spaces and rhythms.

In one way it would have even been safer to come home with Laz. Deana was prepared for devilish tricks, eventually, the energy would change and there would be a good enough reason to make him leave. Even chase him out with the 9mm Glock she had to buy if it came down to it, not that she would waste the bullet.

Never could get enough of Parker. They kept her the focus all night and in time she realized it kept her at a distance. The only sure way to best Parker was to just say no. Deana lost the moment she saw them. Adrenaline was the best aphrodisiac. They were exciting together. Tonight, she would be all but worshiped, and with the rising sun, the fantasy would likely end.

Parker, surprisingly, pulled away sooner than expected. "It seems like you were pretty sure you wanted to go home with him earlier."

Deana gloated internally at their genuine jealousy. "I told you it was just a hookup. It's been a while for me. I'm not stupid enough to get back with a toxic ex."

Parker cringed.

"I didn't mean you..." maybe she was glad they thought so, "but this *is* just a hookup."

"Whatever you say..." The bitterness was back for a moment to break up their peace, but they both loosened up with each kiss and did not let it strain the pleasure that followed.

Late in the darkness, they lay tangled in covers and one another. Blinds cutting off yellow light through the window striped the bed. Deana thought about how easy it could be for this moment to slip right through her fingers, and how many ways love could be snatched from her this time.

"Parker?" They mumbled back affirmatively. "That feeling... or whatever it is you get, when you know something is off..."

The understanding made them more conscious they stirred. "... Yeah?"

"Never ignore that again."

"I promise." They kissed her shoulder.

She rested believing that was a promise they could keep.

☐

Laz watched as they ran up the steps laughing like children and spent some time inside too quiet for his comfort. A little old woman, simple enough to use with so many prescriptions, provided an inconspicuous perspective. Listening at their shared wall in this body would seem nosy, lonely, harmless. He waited hopelessly for the one who was not Deana to come back out, they did not.

He stayed and listened for the door to open again, tormenting himself with the sounds of pleasure and crying. There were tears of reunion on one side of the wall and his own of devastation on the other. He punched at the shared wall. It did not make a sound but broke the borrowed and fragile hand. He wailed and left the old woman's feeble body.

By the time he returned his attention to Red, she was lost to him again. He sensed around for her loathsome energy and there was nothing of her near either nightclub. She was nowhere near Q or Deana and that had to satisfy him tonight. He was depleted. It might be days, he thought, before he could restore his energy to its full potential. It would not take much effort at all to end Red. Maybe as simple as snuffing out the frat. He just had to get to her.

☐

Saturday:

Deana rose early and naturally with the sun shining down its approval. She soaked in Parker's loving feelings, no doubt from sweet dreams. For now, she let the old emotions reawaken, apparently never really gone, and humored the idea of Parker being around for a while at least. She slipped out of bed to prepare a spread to celebrate their however temporary truce.

Turning on the television in view of the kitchen, she half-listened to the Merman's pre-trial updates and mixed batter for pancakes. "The *tail* that's captivating national attention will be the first to include a jury of individuals who have identified themselves to the court as Anomalous." The on-sight newscaster reported as protesters outside of the courthouse held signs in favor and welcome or distaste of the magically inclined. "Their identities and the quantity will be kept private for their safety."

The other newscaster chimed in from a studio as Deana oiled a warm pan, "So many arguable details in this case. If jail time is required, he could be sent to a facility for the Anomalous. Is that correct, Solana?" asked the reporter.

"That is a possibility, Jim. The court must determine if he is in fact *considered* Anomalous. In which case, if he is found guilty, he could be incarcerated along with possibly *dangerous* magical beings. Many of them have been charged with assault with a deadly weapon or force as a result of their power surges."

"Wow!" Said Jim.

Do you think his ability classifies him as Anomalous, Jim?" Solana asked.

"Well, he certainly isn't a psychic," he laughed. "Not as far as we can tell."

If not for the blissful sensations she mimicked from lying with Parker all night, Deana would have been glued to the television distracting herself from loneliness. Today she held dearly to her bliss. Smiling. Singing. Deana ladled in the test pancake as national segments played in the background lightly. She washed and dried a spatula thinking of how last night was just what she needed and she would surrender to what came next.

As if in response a break came in the news. Another live stream came in reported by another local reporter in a familiar-looking alley, "Rezestra claims the life of a community leader and the son that was sure to continue his legacy. I regret to report local restaurateur, Alvin "Al" Rogers and son Al Jr. were found this morning in an alley near Club Mynx..."

Suddenly deaf to the reporter's voice, she looked up and saw the two men. A photo of each of them smiling outside of AJ's graduation ceremony.

"P... Pa..." She struggled to find the breath to yell for them. "Parker!" she managed to stammer.

"Smells good," they said rubbing tired eyes as they entered the living area. Seeing her frozen face they asked, "What's wrong?" She did not answer nor look their way. They followed her line of sight to the TV and saw the two men smiling in the photo. Finally, Parker took in the words of the reporter who told of how the Rogers must have been killed by some amateur, because only a novice would use such a large quantity of the expensive, illicit substance, typically, not wanting to kill victims until they are robbed of all use to captors.

"Besides personal effects that would have been on them, Al's wife reports nothing more was stolen. The family is taking precautions to secure their assets in case any information was given up to the offending party which has yet to be identified. Mrs. Rogers is offering a reward for information that leads to the arrest of the person or persons responsible for the murder of her husband and son. Witnesses saw the two leaving with a woman, but no one knows her whereabouts. They assume that she may have been kidnapped right under their noses."

☐

Saturday, Laz slept until the late hours, waking only to relieve himself. It was already night when he awoke covered in sweat. He went to the kitchen and dowsed frigid water on his face to stay alert. He crawled to the couch famished and longing for days not long ago when he would be force fed by someone's apprentice who might conjure up something to revitalize him and then let him settle back into a food coma.

He had just enough energy to separate himself, but not enough to go on any mission. He had gotten too much of a good thing, needed a day off from his most tiresome gimmick. He felt like he did after the end of a binge. However, Laz thought if he could make himself shower, he could go in his own flesh to look for his target. He might have missed Red, but no one can say he did not look. When he got there, he tried to sense her in the building or close by, but he was not himself yet. He heard that Red was on an errand, but no present minds held details that he could access.

Another drink or two, as a cover he told himself. Everyone seemed like they had control over their actions, scheming and making decisions without her there, but he was not willing to test their minds too much in the state he was in.

When Q spotted him, he stared wondering what he was up to, but he did not engage. Q did not seem perturbed. Laz delicately tiptoed around his loose thoughts taking anything he could reach unobstructed by the blockages. Q had roughed up a few people, gotten violent. He kept his sex workers self-dosing, following him, servicing him, and he still had not been home. He was getting to be too much like Red too soon.

Laz could not take much more. Red was as good as dead. If killing her did not fix Q, he was ready to kill him too. He stayed a while too tired to hike back home. He decided to use the rest of his hardly replenished power to persuade someone pretty and drunk to give up their keys, let him drive, and stay over. Seeing as things were not happening with Deana.

He drove himself to the house of a nameless woman. He compelled her to let him stay, but the sex was her creation. For once he would have happily slept through the night. Desperately needed to. And after round three he thought she would let him, but she sobered up after sweaty sessions of passionless sex leaving him overly exhausted and headed home before the light of day. Sunday, he slept in the entire day. Glad not to be hungover. He did not bother to see the sun and counted his blessings that Siren closed on Sundays.

He worried for a time what another day might do to Q, but too tired he rationalized: The Q he saw last night did not deserve his help he told himself. He held on to hope for the version he knew up until recently, the almost saintly kid. He had to try one last idea and hoped to get Q to come over the old fashion way. Maybe talk to him one on one. He made another order, something to get him through the week. Extra pay if he brought him something to eat.

An hour later, his package and dinner arrived, but Q sent someone else. Someone he did not know to the place he should not be staying. Their connection was severed. Q had to give this kid the address, or someone who knew what he knew. Laz decided to take that to mean that at least Q was alive, but not wanting Laz checking in and chaperoning him and Laz did not have the energy to fight tonight anyhow.

There was food. Not handled with care, but Q made it happen. Laz tipped the man more than enough to cover the extra expenses. He sent him away into the night and began to reunite with the exact drug he tried to save Q from only two days before.

Laz tripped solo. Enjoyed the normal human pleasures of music and masturbation on repeat. He missed this high, but it did not last and was not worth many of the effects. For a moment it was better than he remembered, but he crashed hard after the quick and cheap afternoon.

Monday, just before noon, he dared to go out in the sun. He showered, borrowed sunglasses he found in the house and a clean casual look in which to disappear on the city streets. At a convenience store, he bought a day-old paper at the sight of two grinning and familiar-looking corpses. The normal pallor of death staved off by the effects of Rezestra temporarily preserving them, but they were stiffened by rigor mortis with an unmistakably dead stare. He could not immediately place the men, but knew he needed to remember. He thought back to the year before because it felt like ages since he had seen them.

Too tired to think much for a moment he paid for the paper and a coffee and put it out of his mind for now. It took him walking an identical cement sidewalk struggling to control his own tired legs as he had struggled to control someone else's then. He remembered, dropped his coffee, and frantically skimmed the front-page article.

He realized he had walked past the man's restaurant before. He stood outside of it as a homeless man. He saw Deana there. He had seen that man give him food and then later saw him make sure Deana got home safely. The man sacrificed himself for her and now, Laz feared Deana was still a target. If Red was the mage that Laz thought she was, Deana was still a target. He needed to get to her. He ran.

He failed to think about what he would say if she were home, how he would explain knowing where she lived. He decided to tell the truth if she answered. He knocked, but soon after he could sense that no one was inside, alive or dead. For a moment he knew she was at work and let it bring him peace, but then wondered if Deana was Red's weekend errand.

He was gravely concerned that Red could have found her over the last few days as he slept. She could already have Deana working corners or killed for being able to tie her to the dead men or possibly mentally intruded on by sentient spores. He wondered to himself if he could kill her too if she changed or would he let her become one of Red's creations. He spiraled and decided to get out of view in case she came home. Laz stayed close by atop a nearby building with her apartment entrance still in view. He branched himself a multitude of ways to search for her, not yet at peak strength, but close. No doubt the toxins he ingested over the weekend did not help, but more than it drained him, it appeased him to look.

He spent time in many minds, a minute or maybe a few, just to be sure it was not her. He did not want to deplete his energy too soon, so he tried the easy thing. Magically easy, emotionally terrifying. It was like a refreshing warm-up. Like his first-time trick or treating alone in the cool autumn evening. Fun meeting fear. A dopamine-inducing treat to wind up the corpses like toys and send them his way, with a possible trick of one of the faces being too familiar, but he needed to know and could not just wait.

The dead did not think. The only way to identify a corpse would be to see it. He felt them all over the city, unclaimed, well hidden, fresh, temporarily preserved, and even ice-cold as if from the morgue. He sent them marching like soldiers toward him as he searched for the next and the next.

Hour by hour, body by body, he narrowed down where Deana was not. And let the bodies stop in the street below him exactly where they were when he realized they were not the object of his obsession. Seeing even the Rogers men who died for her. He watched for the woman called Red to make sure she would not come hoping to abduct Deana if she hadn't already, but based on their date Friday, she should have been home by this time. Yet if she were dead and, in the tri-city area, he would have found her among the dozens and dozens of bodies.

We Rejoice in Our Sufferings

The scream of the smoke alarm pierced through the shock and got Parker's attention first. Deana was standing above a cloud of smoke coughing but uncomprehending, and not yet preventing the coming fire. Parker covered the burning pan with another. Deana came back to Earth and grabbed a cookie sheet to fan the smoke detector.

"Sorry, about that," she whispered blaming herself, eyes beginning to well.

Her Saturday and Sunday were tear-filled. After taking in the news, they both spent a little while going through the stages of grief. Starting with heavy denial and bargaining. Parker was unbelieving and Deana thought it should have been her.

"It so easily could have been," she repeated getting quieter each time. She hated to believe that if they stuck together, they would have all gone home alive. "We should have stayed together," she said loud enough for Parker to hear.

They discussed possibilities about the woman, Gina. If she was a victim like the news speculated or if she were the cause of their deaths. Parker did get that feeling, Deana recalled but said nothing. Their guilt told her they were thinking it. She had reached her guilt limit as well.

Instead of unpacking the theory, Deana asked Parker to give her some time to process alone, and Parker's relief was noted. They promised to call and gave a new number – they always had a new number.

☐

Deana showed up for work on Monday disheveled and a little late, vowing to herself to never go out again. The sex was much needed, but not worth anyone's life. At the end of work, Deana heard the door open and clacking heels but did not feel the rush of severe depression that followed most clients into the grief counseling practice.

In a blackish-red mini dress, long coat, and matching veil, Gina came in for the last appointment. The slot her boss reserved for emergencies. Dr. Stevens did the same thing, but at 7 AM. Deana almost took one today, to tell someone that it felt like she had been orphaned again, but decided, much as she needed to talk, she was too far removed from the victim to take up the emergency session.

Gina shuddered at the sight of Deana, inhaled, and exhaled deeply. Deana did not breathe. She stared at the alabaster woman dressed as a widow, but there was too much to say. The doctor was there a second later, punctual. Right on time to keep this woman away for a moment, but an hour later the woman came out dabbing her wet eyes and the doctor wished her a good evening. She traipsed over to the desk where Deana sat.

"Excuse me, you're that young lady I met the other night outside of Mynx."

Deana could see underneath her veil the woman had bruising under her eye, maybe a couple of days healed. "Yes. Ma'am that was me."

"You were with Mr. Rogers. Al, and his son."

81

"Right."

"That's what I came to talk about today."

Deana chose, for now, to think the woman innocent enough to need counseling, but still blamed her for being alive when she had made them stay. Easier than blaming herself. "Would you like to set up a follow-up appointment?" She said struggling to steady her voice.

"Not just yet. I was thinking... this was great, but I would much rather talk to someone a little more familiar with the situation. You see, I am blanking on much of the night, and it just sort of seems like fate that we're both here. Maybe I could buy you dinner or –"

"Oh... I don't know..."

"...I understand if you don't feel comfortable seeing me. You must think this is my fault."

"I don't... I... dinner sounds... nice." Deana's shoulders dropped on the last word.

"Fantastic!" She sat down in the waiting room. "I'll wait here for you."

Normally, Deana left work and bussed home, but Gina got them to dinner in luxury. A hot red convertible of course. Some classic, stylish, ubiquitous thing. The restaurant was classier as well although much more inconspicuous. The drinks were bottled and opened at the table to prove safe to diners, ensuring them that no Rezestra crime rings could exist here, as the wealthy were easily targeted through fine dining.

They just talked, only interrupted by the waiter, "Welcome ladies, my name is Eli. I will be your server this evening."

Red kept ordering drinks for them. Unshared bottles, sparkling water for Deana, and dry reds for Gina. By the top of their second bottles, Deana thought maybe Gina may have been sloshed enough to divulge information more carelessly. Feeling nothing of her still, Deana presented the facts as she understood them, "They were fine when I left them with you. How is it you and I are having dinner tonight and they OD on *Rezestra* after *you* –"

"– Hey, I only went out to have a fun time," she said with a heavy tongue, "I wanted to spread some cheer, but we were *all* drugged. We were dancing, some guy asks us if we wanted to party. I bought us drinks, and he had some... other party favors, but we were having a *fun time!*" She took another sip of wine, "I was living my eighties, prom-queen-dream again, and then... I must have blacked out, because I can hardly remember anything else.

"Flashes of what happened afterward come and go. I remember pouring something into a glass and then nothing until the next morning. I did not know that anyone died until I saw it in the paper. I hate to think that I may have helped someone take advantage of us, kill such kind and innocent people." She sobbed "... I thought for sure I would be safe with your friends protecting me, but... then on the front page... I .... I...."

She was inconsolable. Deana thought she sounded like the early victims of Rezestra. She wondered how this woman could be so careless with strangers having the same information as everyone. Then she remembered she was arguably more reckless that same night. The woman was drunk and emotional, but Deana could not let up until she got all the answers she could, "They were found in the alley... where did you wake up?"

"I was in an alley too, another one close by. Missing my money, my cigarettes. my..." she covered her face, "my panties... I don't know who, but someone raped me. The worst part is, I couldn't even put up a fight. I probably let it happen. I probably thanked them."

"Oh god..." Deana huffed. The words jabbed her heart. "I can't even imagine. I am so sorry. I... My boss mostly specializes in grief counseling... I mean... I know you're grieving too, but if you want a number for someone to talk to about ..."

"No... no... I was hoping to get laid, I just... I wish I had a choice... that I was aware. Horrible as it is to think someone had their way with me, I got to walk away while Al and AJ were killed."

"Survivor's guilt. I've also been feeling it ever since. I left that night so I could feel safe at home, and now I wonder if I could have kept them safe just by being there. I have to live with that." Deana's lip twitched then.

"I'll probably be in therapy a while personally," Gina started, "but I think it's better than therapy being able to talk to you. Thanks. I didn't even know them. But of course, the guilt... and... I guess the tragedy of how it happened kind of reminds me of what happened to my grandmother when I was a girl.

"I was nine when she died. My first experience with death. I knew it would happen eventually, but she was not even that old. She still had plenty of life in her, but my mother and I were on the way to bring her a basket we made. I drew pictures, and my mom made her favorite oatmeal cookies and baked bread... I was so excited I ran to the door long before my mom even got the basket out of the car.

"She knew we were coming, and the door was always unlocked. So, I was not surprised that it was even cracked by the time I got to it. I pushed it, I called out to her, but she didn't answer. I thought she was hiding, but when I got in the living room. I saw her body lying on the floor.... her skin was cut from her." She sobbed, "I screamed... the back door slammed, and my mother ran in.

"Later it was said that some crazy brute cut her skin off to keep with others he cleaned and dried. She was not his first victim. If we were only fifteen, twenty minutes earlier... I could have scared him off and she would have lived. I may have been a victim too had I been there, but...Talk about survivor's guilt."

There was a moment of silence broken by Gina. "Do you mind driving?"

"No problem." Deana agreed.

"Good. Waiter!" She ordered another bottle and dessert for them both. By the end of two blondies a la mode, Deana had gone from sorry for Gina to amused by her. Her voice, deepened from two decades of smoking, gave her the range to sing the bass notes to "Under the Boardwalk" poorly. It felt like such a rare thing to sing and laugh. Deana grinned dramatically and Gina paid the tab.

The valet brought the car back around, top-up, and Deana helped its tipsy and belting owner into the passenger side safely.

As soon as she got in the woman asked, "Do you mind stopping by Siren?"

Deana did not remember responding. Pulling up to the sign at the back entry and parking in the owner's reserved space, was the last retrievable image to stain her mind.

□

The bodies made the living flee. Red likely would not come this way on foot but might be brave enough to drive by. He scanned the living who passed in cars for a sign of either of them. She was not at Siren, nor had she passed by yet.

He could not think of another place to look except for everywhere. It had been more than two days since the restaurant owner died. Deana could be just about anywhere. He had a choice to make, search everyone in the city hoping she was still in it and almost definitely run out of juice before finding her or keep his radius confined to conserve energy. This was Deana. Failing was not an option.

About three hours after she should have been back, he sensed something repulsive and familiar. It was pushing him away, making it almost untraceable, keeping him at bay from just outside of where he had been searching for it. In trying to create a shield between itself and him, he was alerted to Red's presence. A bright red car flashed across the street where the signal he sensed radiated from. In working to inspect the minds in the car, his energy circled hers, tailing it, refusing to lose her again. It was too much to try and hold on to her and like a savior to his weakened energy, Deana made her presence known.

She could not have been aware of sensing him first, but she surprised him. His energy in the car, changing the mood, piqued her interest and he felt her presence, also familiar, but more inviting. It was her, still there appearing conscious, but only following orders on autopilot. It only mattered that she was alive, but as a bonus she was wide open to him. Rezestra-dosed, but not a lethal amount. It impressed him that it did not inhibit her ability to drive. He rejoiced that there were no spores in her mind, but still Red controlled her keeping her alive for now. He took shelter there.

Without being close enough to protect her physically, he would have to rely on being able to make her protect herself, helping her to lie if needed, helping her not say too much while still playing the part, and not a moment too soon.

Through Deana he heard Red ask her if she were a "nasty girl."

'*No!*' he made her change her initial answer at the last second. He held on to Deana's energy and urgently raced to ground level to run behind the car on foot. Even at night, he would be able to spot the red car. They headed back to where he guessed they might go, back to where Red first saw Deana, back to Siren. The leech types always keep a hive for their possessions, but he needed to be certain. The horde gave him cover, at best he appeared to be running away from them to safety as he tailed the car, and he did not have to pretend to be afraid. He hoped this might be enough to take attention away from him being a black man running at night.

He would not stop to explain his running to anyone. The truth would get him classed as Anomalous and too empowered. They would have to put him down, as there was no way they could contain him. He would learn after all if the B.R.A.D agency could take out a mage like him.

He could call the unit himself on Red. She had the power and the illegal activity, but they could raid the whole place taking casualties to get to her, and that could not include Deana. So, he ran and stayed in her mind using his vision and Deana's toward Siren, the double sight draining him twice as fast.

He ran for Deana and felt as if he were running in the traffic as well as on the sidewalk. His brain tried making sense of the two sets of imagery and his feet wanted to stop for brake lights ahead while he sprinted over cracked and uneven terrain on his own path.

Plans for Welfare and Not for Evil

Red wanted the girl as soon as she saw her at Siren. Red glossed over her once and then twice, the third time Red could not ignore the feeling. It was not like with the guys. She was driven madly to them like dinner only to be hungry again and again. But the girl was a hunch that suggested taking all these men and not this one real treasure was a mistake. Red would not die if she did not take her like she feared she might with her male prey, but it would be a loss. At the very least she could earn a pretty penny.

Red became aware of another drawn to Siren Friday night who stirred her intuitive detector. The girl sat with a man almost as beautiful as she was. More handsome than those she collected. A slim built guy, smaller than her usual type, with a pretty face and hard body, light brown skin, and soft, billowy hair. He may have been her same height. Red was a taller woman, but that didn't make him that tall of a man, yet his looks intrigued her. She would have marked him as hers and called him back when it was time to feed if not for the feeling that she would be risking her own fate. From a distance, it felt as if she were safe, but close to him or alone, she did not know what might happen.

For a moment conceited with the power she once referred to as an affliction, she planned a sneakier way to capture them both, but when the dreaded god of man eventually caught her watching their table, specifically at his date, Red saw more clearly the promise of her death in his stare. The little man somehow fired a strike to her mind that sent her eyes shooting back until they showed only white.

Stupefied for a moment, she did not know how her new powers

must have reacted, but when she could see again, the young man was down. Afraid she would not be able to recreate whatever she had done in retaliation, she disappeared and let the girl go only regretting the dissatisfaction of her curiosity.

Red had one more club, Mynx. The first one she "had to have," and Big Daddy bought it for her, then took it back in the divorce. Her new powers helped her reclaim it. She contemplated keeping him along with his every asset leaving him a financially and sexually drained vegetable, but there was then no need to keep him alive siphoning her power, making trouble for her as he changed. She was unconcerned as to what happened to him after she shared the thought to her collective that she wanted him dead and gone.

Mynx thrived and there was bound to be someone special among the immense crowed. She had not made it inside yet two of her earlier captives were outside smoking, exchanging laughs, and cutting up as she watched passersby. She pulled a few off the street and promised them pleasures inside or marked them for later. Just as she settled for ordinary prey and thought to go inside, she saw her treasure walking right up to her and the grim reaper nowhere in sight.

The girl was now with three people, but none of them seemed like they would tamper with her fate. Red tried her same tricks. It worked on almost everyone, but none were so desired. All of them planned to cut their night short, but the men proved easy to persuade with a simple touch and intent. Just like that she downloaded all that they knew about '... *Deana.*' Next for the gender-less looking one with the kind eyes and quiet disposition, '*Parker.*' Red had them on the hook and only a few steps away from entering her den. She could have them with one laced drink, but the girl, it seemed, was on to her.

Red hoped her power would easily travel like a current through them both with one touch and a bit of confidence, but she would not learn tonight. Not with them. She only managed to capture Al and AJ. They did have some fun at first, even though she could tell they did not understand why they could not refuse it. She and Al danced for a while before she snuck off to feed on AJ.

She made them both drink shot after shot of Henny and Rere and as it made its way through them, she got off on making old Al have a bump with her and when he felt the high rush in, she dared him to punch her in the face, hard. The black eye and bits of information they had on the girl were all she needed from them. She would find Deana's place or job, or as a last resort, she would see her at their funeral.

Rezestra made the men pleasant. In their final moments, they smiled so hard it had to hurt. The corners of their mouths cracked from the frigid air and pressure. Still, under her spell, she only needed to wish for them to be fun, and they would be. She wanted them to stay in the alley and lay still and quiet once it stopped being amusing. They got down onto the damp and dirty gravel and began to drift into extremely euphoric death with their compliance giving her a clean and nearly untraceable escape. Deana was now a target of desire as well as a loose end to tie up.

She spent the next couple of days trying to find where Deana worked exactly, that and hiding from the guy who wanted to keep them apart. Q informed Red through their connection that he had returned to Siren on Saturday. Laz was his name, someone Q liked in his past life who very well could have been the threat he seemed to be. So, she stayed away unable to ignore the instinct again. It kept her alive showing her the ropes of her power and influence, keeping her fed magically, sexually, and her ego flourishing. She did not exactly know where Deana lived but did not risk Laz being there either. She decided to try her at work.

Al and AJ knew Deana's job title but not where she was
employed. They heard her mention she bussed to and from and Red
narrowed it down based on busses that stopped near the clubs and in
the radius of a psych office. It took a bit of doing, but by Monday
she knew where to be and planned to get in the same day by any
means. Red ran the risk of the girl calling the cops before the end of
the session, but she would have to really be sure Red was guilty or
she would be risking the integrity of the practice having the police
after her. She decided to play the innocent victim for the doctor and
Deana both.

Red wanted her for keeps. Intended to make her give herself
daily double doses to keep her pretty, fresh, and obedient, make her
the best friend she always wanted. Like the ones she used to have
when her waist was just as small.

She knew where to take her. No one Red knew of could resist a
luxe dining experience all expenses paid. The girl would more than
pay-off a long and extravagant dinner. Red did not quite own this
place, but she had celebrated the finality of her divorce here and
gotten a dose of Rezestra in this place where they have advertised
taking every precaution for that not to happen. These careful venues
were perfect for The Great Eli to do his best work.

Like any drug, it did not quite work the same on Red but to
keep her looking good. She would not have known if not for the
waiter politely asking for a tip of a certain amount and telling her
not to tell anyone he said so. He was gloved and she could not touch
him casually, but on a feeling, she paid what he asked and patiently
waited for him to leave for the night.

Approaching him as he left, she seduced him like she was

made to do. It did not matter that he was not into women. She had chosen him, and he'd be unable to move though he wouldn't realize. She touched him with her captivating touch to make his mind hers. She saw herself as a young boy practicing novelty magic like a stage magician. Performing before toy dinosaurs and stuffed zoo animals collected as tokens from different traveling shows. Far as he knew he was not Anomalous, but he was determined to be great.

"Well," she told him then, "I will give you a chance to put on masterful performances for me."

Not Anomalous, but a worthy tool. She let him continue his sleight of hand dosing of anyone she came into the restaurant with. Under her influence, she did not have to share at all, but she made sure he took care of himself so he could be used repeatedly.

She acted alongside him, playing drunk well enough to make it look to the restaurant-goers and staff that she needed a ride, but Deana was hers before dessert. Once in the car, Red looked at Deana from the passenger's seat, "We're gonna wait until you get a lot friendlier," she began, "and then you're going to make us some money." Deana started the engine and headed toward Siren unconcerned on the surface.

"Out of the way!" Red yelled to a pedestrian in the road. Ashes spilled from her cigarette as she cursed through tight lips. She took it out of her mouth sticking her head out of the window. "Entitled asshole!" she yelled to the man as they passed. "Just like my ex-husband... my *late* ex-husband," she said rolling the window back up.

"He liked to say things like, 'It's in a man's nature to want to spread his seed, babe.' Why he thought his sperm was such a gift I will never know – stumpy, hairy, ignorant fuck. I would tell him,

'Sure hon,' and remind him it's in a woman's nature to look for better options. You know, better protector of the children and provider of food, that sort of thing." She took another drag. "I told that filthy bastard that every woman is entitled to an upgrade as much as any man is entitled to spread his precious seed. He didn't like that." She smiled. "He shut up about the other women, although I know he didn't quit them, but he did provide more. I got Mynx and he had a few too, I'm sure." It was quiet before she continued, "Who let men run the world anyway?"

In her condition, Deana could not discern that the question was rhetorical. "They beat us until we let them have it." She answered unexpectedly.

Red was stunned silent. She contemplated. "You're probably right," she said low, and then chuckled. Louder she added, "No way in hell they got it using their brains." Red laughed until she choked. Deana laughed too. "You so get it, Deana. I think if you and I got a chance to get to know one another, we'd be good pals. I don't have the best track record with my girlfriends. Made a lot of guy friends though, and it's getting easier and easier. I have a gaggle of them working for me, didn't exactly need powers for that, but now I can train them well, like Eli.

"You know, the story about my grandma? That was just my twisted version of Little Red Riding Hood... The story of little Red, get it? Just buying some time. You see the women in my little family, I only use Rezestra to keep them around. Magically they don't feed me, and I can always give them back their free will. We party, I make sure they're having fun, but it'd be nice to have a real friend to share this with. I figure it's got to be someone special. Then you walk into Siren feeling like... like a twice in a row lottery win. I'd like to be able to trust you, Deana.

"We could be like sisters! In the meantime, Rezestra is not so bad. My women get to spend their hours living out their dirtiest fantasies for high-end clientele, politicians and traveling men with too much money. No regrets, just their own idea of fun, and they get paid for it! Top dollar too." She lit another cigarette. Dragged and exhaled. "Are you a nasty girl Deana?" She asked hopefully.

"Ye– no." she corrected.

"Oh, come on, I saw you with that hot piece you came to Siren with the other night. You tellin' me you never get dirty for him?" Red did not wait for the answer. "Well, I guess you can't exactly lie to me." She squirmed uncomfortably in her chair. "I was wondering about him... he makes me uneasy. One of my guys said he was around again this Saturday, but he doesn't have one useful bit of information on the guy. Except for his name." She puffed. "I think it's a fake. I should know. You know his real name?"

"Laz."

"Hm... maybe. I'm getting the creeps just thinking about him."

Just then Deana slowed the car as an increasing number of people walked congesting the road.

"What is this, a fucking parade?" Red reached over honking the horn. They were not far from Mynx when they noticed no other cars on the street. She squinted her eyes peering deeper out of the front windshield, spine-tingling as she noticed not all the bodies were walking, many laid in the street deathly still.

'*He's coming.*' She thought.

Between two apartment buildings, the undead collected in piles blocking the road. Uninhabited bodies limped to the spot collapsing onto one another adding to the pile. Deana seemed aware of the moment and halted the car just there, her foot on the break.

Paranoia crept up on Red, "What are you doing? Drive!" Deana did not move. A person lay in front of the car where they could both plainly see washed in the light of the car beams. Behind them, illuminated in brake lights, more figures approached prowling toward the Cadillac. Red's heart pounded, terrified, feeling the promise of death in the air as it teased her with a morbid march. This time she shouted it, "Drive!"

Deana floored the accelerator and went over the body of a young woman as if she were a speed bump. She drove slowly creeping up the road, winding the car left and right to avoid hitting bodies when she could, but not stopping again.

☐

They arrived at Siren entering through the back and into Red's new office. Q waited standing. "We got a buyer for her."

"Already? I just got her."

"He just got here too, calls himself a collector and he's been hoping to get '*it*' while it's under control."

"How did he know we had her under control?"

Q shrugged.

"Fine. Bring him in and stay close by me." She told Deana to sit in the corner of the room.

Red met the slick man and offered him any other girl, "She's kind of a new toy. You understand."

"If I were a betting man, and I am, I'd say you know that none of the others are going to compare."

His interest was more confirmation. She still had Deana thus still had the upper hand. There was no way Red would share her ignorance. She hoped her luck would be enough.

At his first ridiculous offer of seven hundred and fifty thousand dollars, Red held her composure and said, "I wouldn't rent her to you for that price." A bluff, but the mysterious collector's pricey interest in combo with her hunch, enticed her to push him for all she could to make it worth it.

He laughed amused, displaying a golden tooth. "Name your price."

☐

Laz reached a new level of exhaustion pounding pavement, retaining the overlapping views. Deana confirmed their destination as Siren came into her perspective behind the wheel. He held her vision long enough to be sure they would go in. The two walked in inconspicuously through the back entrance.

Unsure of how to get in, he sent her a calming message, *'Everything is going to be okay.'* Rezestra helped her believe. *'I am coming.'*

He released her perspective, taking the much-needed break from holding her view to rest his aching mind, his body feeling lighter too. Almost fully detached, he could not quite let go completely as he heard an unfamiliar voice in the room.

"Your club seems to attract a certain type," a man said. His voice sounded as if he were in Laz's ear. He was inspecting Deana like she was a product or show dog, clearly not caring about boundaries or the muscle Red had in place. "I wasn't expecting it to be female. She is very pretty. Have you gained her loyalty yet?"

"Not yet," another bluff from Red.

His voice a sly whisper, "What's your name pretty?"

She spoke mechanically. "Deana."

Laz sent the input, *'Answer him slower,'* He needed the time.

"Stand up." the man said as if she were a trained pet.

'Slowly!' The quiet became unbearable for Laz, but he pushed on using borrowed strength. He could see the squat building where it all began, but it still seemed miles away.

There was a labored breathing in his ear. The same man. He muttered to her now, "What's your power, Deana?"

"Wait," It was Red sounding impatient, "She isn't yours until I get the cash." curious she added, "...what makes you think she has power?"

"I don't think, my dear. I know. *That* is my power, and if you haven't noticed, Siren is very... alluring to our types. That includes you."

"You know about my power?"

"Mm, yes. I don't know what it is, but it's manifested in you recently, like many others. What an exciting time for me to be alive. This one however... it's only showing psychic abilities for now, but I have a good feeling."

"You too?" Red asked, glad the collector was experiencing the same thing as herself around Deana.

The man then turned his interest to Red, "Oh you *are* a prize." He offered to buy her as well, "A job we'll call it."

Laz heard the collector try to make the deal sweeter, buy the girl and hire Red for a regular and equally absurd salary. When he asked her about her power, Laz checked out. It gave him time to get to Siren, but he could not get to where she was.

The bar was opened to dining this night and the music was lowered to suit its Monday night quiescence. Still, the door beneath the VIP was guarded although the front door was not. The bouncer was sober, and one whom Laz could not tempt with all the money in his pocket thanks to Red's venom. He let Deana know telepathically that he could not easily get to her, he could not control or even bend the poisoned bouncer. *'New plan,'* he alerted. *'I'll find a way to help you save yourself.'*

You Shall Eat and Not be Satisfied

The collector was filthy rich. He had clearly snapped or gone crazy, as far as Red thought.

"So, you got a feeling about her," The man said, "what about me?"

"No. I wouldn't have guessed."

"Hmm, how did you get her?"

Red told him about the waiter and his sleight of hand act. How she hexed him and used him to get Deana dosed.

"So simple and elegant. You *have* to come work for me!"

"Why?"

"As I've said I am a collector. You are a *must* have."

"I'm not for sale."

"Already you are a slave, and I am offering you pay for your burdens."

"You don't know me. *I* am free as a bird on the fourth of July, honey."

"Why then did you go through so much trouble to get this

girl?"

"I told you, I had a feeling."

"And it's driving you. You're a slave to it. Your power told you that you had to take the waiter or someone fast, am I right? And then you had to keep him and have the girl on a hunch. You didn't make those choices. Your power did. Sorry dear, happens to the best of us. At least I'm offering you compensation to be what you are."

She spoke firmly. "I'm *not* for sale."

"Very well, It's her I'm here for." He resumed fondling the girl, smelling her, and intermittently looking up at Red while he did so.

"Show us what you can do then, Deana." Red commanded.

"No! Don't! The collector said in haste. "It's one thing to ask *about* the power, but to ask for demonstrations can be lethal. I learned that the hard way." He lifted a pant leg to show a metallic lower leg. "Lucky for you she doesn't have full use of her power yet."

☐

Laz sat at the bar after he realized he would have to kill the guard or fool him and Red both. Either choice could get others killed as well; could get Deana killed. He could not make them help her or even make them want to, and settled for her view afraid to alert the collector. A legendarily determined type.

Instead, he floated in and out to watch and think, ordered a bottle, ordered the dead outside of her apartment to Siren. Just a few of the closest ones to guard the exit Red used to escape him before.

He would make a scene if necessary and kill her in her nearly empty dining room. He flashed an image of Deana's face to the horde of departed. She was not to be touched, but anyone with her was not to leave the place alive. He was careful to choose corpses who still had eyes. Hard as it was, he did not risk a drink tonight.

It scared him that Deana was the only one in the room susceptible to him. Only once in his life had he ever experienced such a predicament and then he was certain he was good as dead. Now he questioned what might happen to the love of his life if he tried to make her save herself in a room full of armed and criminal Anomalous that he could not read?

His only hope was that the collector was right. Perhaps there was a power to find here in her mind. He never did have a chance to check and almost wished that she had answered the collector when he asked before.

Aimlessly searching for powers that might not exist made him feel hopeless. He explored her thoughts thoroughly. Plan B was to kill them all risking his freedom and both of their safety to get her out. It was a long shot, but he had to try. Emotional triggers made obvious the merman's ability. If he were lucky, and historically he was not, it would be so simple again. He hoped for warm copper lights as he searched the depths of her being, but becoming a merperson would not help her.

Laz could hear the man give her a bit of distance and ask her to undress.

'Slowly.' Laz demanded again and began looking for memories that could trigger her into power.

Laz's presence brought her comfort and there was a moment of peace in her that she may have been aware of. No doubt she was wearing a wide drugged smile despite the internal chaos. But he could feel the cycle of a Rezestra victim begin again as he felt her forgetting her predicament and the collector's words. She continued to obey the commands given as if her hands had their own mind. They removed her bra automatically. She noted the spectators as if for the first time, realized she could not stop her fingers from unhooking and gasped terrified before forgetting again. Laz would not forget.

New components stirred within her. Powers, he believed. The first of which he captured felt weightless, kind, sweet, and shallow. He discovered it was advancing quickly in her now. She was using it and he could not even tell what was being done. Only that it was adding to her fear. He wanted to stay there in its nurturing ambiance, but its passive nature could not save her.

He heard again another awful command for her echoing in the space. She was naked and still, the collector wanted to see more. She obliged or began to. '*Slowly,*' he added in a telepathic response. He dove deeper beyond the shallow outer magic with no more time to settle in her sight or be hailed by her fear.

'*Fear,*' he thought may have been the answer and he reminded her of her current condition. Something dormant beneath the power she now exercised rustled a bit like it had been nudged. But he could not perceive it yet.

He called forth from her memories fear that he had caused her in the past. No doubt the worst troubles of her life until tonight. He had purged out the night he had reminisced over his mother's betrayals and how he had gotten higher than he should have, any normal person wouldn't have survived. Deana's only fault was that she was there and sounded like his mother used to. She did not know he had the power to manipulate her fear. He had gotten it to a new peak making her cower and beg him to stop before he threw the first punch. He acknowledged the irony. Now that there was good reason to use the ability he inherited from his father on her, he was not close enough to be sure of his aim. For once, it mattered.

A series of similar moments poured, and the dormant ability began to stretch expanding within the interior space of her lesser power. A moment he did not recognize made itself seen. It should have been a fear he caused, but the scene was new to his mind.

My Portion Forever

The memory of the delivery came too familiar to her. She refused the epidural, wanting to be sober for the first minutes of her baby's life, and so suffered the well-preserved recollection. Her eyes pooled before she surrendered herself to forgetting, Rezestra doing quickly what she could not.

☐

The prophecy was true. Deana worked to suppress the scene, but Laz would not miss this moment twice. He pushed more, and though there was resistance from the outer reaches of herself there was no more resistance felt above Laz. He got what he needed; what she needed but did not want.

He unearthed more and more of her deep pain and joy from this greatest moment, and he split himself again as if he had all his strength renewed to bask in her memory too. His only regret was being unable to move into the minds in the room he observed and see her glow as she brought life into their dim world. He watched as if he'd pushed the infant out himself and that was somehow better.

"It's a boy! You have a son," a smiling doctor told him handing him the newborn.

The light that he perceived from the parts of him that pushed felt cold yet smelled of sweat. There were many colors and they had never looked so rich and beautiful. He laughed as he bore witness to it and began to pull himself together. Though he was unable to stay long in the first memories of his offspring, he was in love like these colors could nearly express, but the exhaustion came back harder than before. He had to make a choice it was now more critical to save his child's mother. Save the only mind he knew could help him get to his son.

He needed to stay here, the pushing was done, and he hurt for rest as no man could, but he noticed that the colors and lights faded. the cold and sweat remained... something consumed the joy and welcomed the pain, feasted on the light and all he had managed to dig up was the worst pains of her life. Her most traumatic events were now just beneath her surface. The shadow, as it went, had won after all. He only hoped that it would save her sure to be miserable life.

This second power within her expressed itself as *'feeding'* on the best of her feelings. To Laz it was more sentient and more alive than magic is known to feel, more than Red's hateful orb, but another wicked thinking thing. A force not motivated to save itself, but to destroy others.

Laz spoke to Deana and the unearthed thing as it fed helping him birth itself into existence. It was shadow eating light. Hoping it heard, he thought toward it:

'Have your revenge but let Q live if you can.' And he pictured Q as he was before, hoping that the thing would recognize the humanity he once had, and care to save him. *'I am coming.'*

'I'll try.' was the last transmission he had gotten before the cursed thing pushed him out of this scarce-light space. Deana was no longer in control, but she was still there.

☐

No money had changed hands yet when Red noticed a shift. It was like someone hit a switch inside the girl. Something was different. They both underestimated her.

"On second thought, she's no longer for sale either," Red told the collector.

"You felt that too?" the collector grinned even more impressed with Red, "Well, you should know that now I have a hunch that we should get out of here." He was unafraid, but he ran away limping on the prosthetic leg.

He made for the back door, the one Red and Deana came in, or rather he tried. Laz's horde was in place there when he opened the heavy door. They pushed their way to the man. Grabbing and clawing at him enraged. His screams ricocheted in the cement space as they tore him open. As if in kind, Deana's skin split making room for the hunched and bone-chilling thing she was becoming.

Red watched as the girl nearly doubled in size, her hands elongated ending in talons. Her teeth sharpened and her eyes narrowed. Red was caught in between the mauling dead and a hulking beast. Angel and Q drew their guns ready to shoot if Red desired. Instead, she prayed for Deana's loyalty or that Rezestra might still have use. The creature eyed her approaching, it's breathing heavy and loud.

Red looked into the bleak stare horrified but hoping to reason. "Deana, my girl, I knew you were special. Let's say you and I put our heads together and –"

There was an ungodly noise that rippled from the monster in the room cutting her off.

"Shit!" She yelled, and the being stalked toward her as if it were pleased to force her to inch closer to the undead. As Red's back got nearer to the exit they blocked, one of the animated corpses snapped it's head up angrily at Red. Deana's beastly form quickened and snatched the woman up into it's gigantic hand. She screamed and both of her minions shot aiming at the bloodthirsty being.

□

His consciousness was hers, but his body had been resting until he came fully and painfully to his tired flesh. He rose blurred vision to the bottle having been lighter than he had left it. Before he could care he heard the guarded door become the concern for the bouncer that he hoped it would: Snarls, cursing, screaming, and shooting that cleared the bar except for Red's underlings and Laz. None of them were to move, the big guard was not to open the door. He knocked, "Is everything alright?" The collective sounds continued, ignoring him, soft music still playing in the dining room. More shots rang out, followed by a guttural roar.

Laz began to think it a mistake to set the attack. If Red did not want the door opened it would not be, but he would have to convince himself not to fear for Deana's life. He could potentially save her especially if she died with him this close, but he has never stayed to see what happened to the people he brought back to life. He would for her if it came to that. He half calmed himself believing her life would be protected by the parasitic magic feeding on her, though at the cost of the irreversible damage to her soul.

Laz was so certain it could be of use though unsure the sacrifice had value. Maybe it would kill every being in the room with it, but what would make it stop there, he wondered. The bouncer was not called in, but he was tempted by round after round of shots. Laz thought Deana must be dead now and sprang up to kill the bouncer and the armed bartender to get to her quickly and revive her while he had the time. He convinced himself that anyone still in the bar needed to die anyway.

Just as he reached for the energies of the two of Red's minions he could see, there was a terrifying rip and the alarming wail of a woman. The guard drew a weapon and opened the door – Red wanted to be saved. With another gun now out for Deana's blood, Laz made for the door, but there was no one for either of them to save.

There were body parts torn from someone that included a metallic leg. Torsos maimed and mangled alongside bitten-off appendages that bled onto the floor of a cement-walled room. Red was mostly intact except for her head apparently detached and rolled just away from the rest of her. Laz was still until one contorted being writhing and screaming broke through the shock. Q propped himself up on his arms, sitting with his legs torn away and discarded. He was alive as requested, half alive, choking, and shouting curses with his final breaths.

The guard was unmovable before, but he desperately wanted to leave. Anyone who was not Laz would want to leave.

Deana and whatever controlled her began moving toward them with exposed skin covered in fresh lacerations. She heaved as if they were all just a warmup. She eyed the two men and calculated.

His eyes stayed glued to her as he spoke to the guard. The suggestion was out loud, no magic. "I'll stay with her if you wanna back out of here... *slowly*." Then to her, he uttered, "I know you can hear me, D. Come back. You're safe."

He chanced a side glance. Seeing Red in pieces tempted him to check the guard's mind and Q – Part of whom was close by screaming in agony mixing in curses at Deana. There were only remnants of her true self visible in this state. She was bigger and stronger now with blood on her teeth and nails and death behind her eyes. Laz knew it to be death sure as he had always seen it. He hoped it was pain that made Q rage and not what lingered of Red.

Deana watched Laz as the guard began to creep backward toward the door which they entered running regrettably too far in guns flailing. Laz wondered terrified if he deserved what was coming next. Whatever Deana was about to do to him, he accepted. He betrayed her more times than anyone, leaving her in damming positions, although arguably less so than tonight. Perhaps this was how they were always meant to end.

□

It sprang forth, hitting the ground hard, running and pouncing. It landed on the guard just as he made it to the opened door. It twisted his neck easily like a soda cap and left him in the door frame for the bartender with the shotgun to see. Turning again to Laz, it eyed him with recognition and confusion. The thing was uncertain if this was its master, or if the woman it was a part of wanted to keep him alive. Being birthed prematurely, it could not yet trust itself to lead. Willingly, it gave in to the woman's desires.

□

He did not dare try to induce fear in her now. Her beast-like frame blockaded one door and the other was too far to escape her speed, he surrendered with one power left to kill, but he would die before trying it on her, even now when he wondered if she were present at all. She crept toward him.

Again, he searched for her energy in the air. Her lip turned up into a snarl sensing him. *'Still beautiful,'* he thought toward the thin wisps of her that remained in the beast. She jerked in response, rolling her neck loosely around. He reached his hand out to the beastly beauty at this moment hoping her aware or vulnerable, or at least in goodbye if it were to be the last feeling. He made contact with her cracked skin.

The shock of old conflicting emotions overwhelmed the confused entity that consumed her. She fainted into his arms. Silence only fended off by Q's agony. Laz caught her and crouched with her still too heavy frame as she shrank back into the size, he had seen her the last time they met at Siren. Gently he lay her on the cold concrete and all that she was began to sleep.

He stayed with her in material body but split himself again just enough to read Q and check what he anticipated. The pins still floated vibrantly within the recesses of his being as if unaware Red were gone. The virus still thrived within his body, her will passed on to him and growing.

"Just wait until I get my hands on you, you rotten bitch! I'll kill you!" He fused through clenched teeth to the sleeping Deana. Declarations he would never live to fulfill. Laz stared at his love and sighed accepting he would have to kill this once good soul who called him the same. That part of Q was gone, or there and infected beyond recognition. Laz accepted that he would need time to make peace with magic and how it might always change the ones he loved and himself too.

Around Deana, he wrapped a hand to sustain life and held on with care. He then raised a hand to make death come too soon.

111

'Quickly,' he thought to himself, now whole, reminding himself that the Q who was all Q did not deserve the suffering he could manifest.

Laz ignored the yelling. He could not look at his associate now. Mourning his life had already begun. Q would be the good version in his memory. Laz felt around in the room for Q's life force and felt the needles stabbing as if they were real, but not stopping him as he turned like a nob, a tight grip that would silence him permanently.

Red still had minions out there, but Deana was safe and for however briefly, they were alone.

She was herself again, physically, and mentally his. None of her wounds were fatal. The blood dripping out of her mouth was not her own and did nothing to stop her from being a vision he thought. Her power, if anything, made her that more lovely in his eyes – a beautiful monster finally fit for him.

He commanded her, "Kiss me like you miss me, D." She rose to embrace him. He put his hand to her neck and for a moment that passion returned that he never expected to feel from her again.

He could not help himself but to further indulge. From her memories he dug to steal a name she'd worked long and hard to block from her thoughts, feeling hopeless with every reminder. Becoming aware of the name, he was pained too. It made her deception even more real. She gasped for air, and he noticed himself squeezing too tightly at her throat. He released her neck and her mind.

"We don't have a lot of time, D. You should get home, unless...." He recalled his chore from The Madam. "I know a sort of... haven. Magic isn't a crime there. You'd be worshiped." He envisioned a life they could start there. "I know about..." he choked up at the name of his progeny, "Icarus." She shuddered tensely and then relaxed, forgetting again at the surface.

"Deana, if you knew what happened tonight... if you remembered my part in all of this, is there a chance that you'd want to come with me to this place?"

Crimson mouth still smiling, now open and wide from chemical euphoria, she shook her head no, almost peaceful after her demonic tantrum, too much so to open her eyes or speak.

His jaw clenched. "Well, you can't sleep here. Get dressed and go home, you can rest there. I'll cover you."

With his remaining power, he reached to the bodies still heading toward her apartment from this direction. He flashed the command for them to wait for her before going ahead. She would appear to be another of the dead walking. It would seem she suffered death by a thousand cuts. If anyone were fool enough to approach her, she would be defended by the dead who walked with her. As a few of them approached Siren, he sent her out with them and stormed off into the shadows alone.

She Who Began Good Work

Tuesday:

Deana came to with the cold taste of metal in her teeth and the alarm clock chirping out confirming it was five in the morning. She smacked it silent. Dreadfully dehydrated she rolled over and dozed back off, a pillow over her head to drown out the sound of early morning traffic and cursing neighbors.

She surfaced slowly from a panic dream and on the way to awakening she remembered trying to stand still, rocking, and almost falling over. An assault of images of faces swirling and vague enjoying her delusion. She remembered hiding her face in her hands and feeling her mouth cemented in a grin that mocked her bulging and teary eyes. There was a realization of a helpless predicament: screams and a white-hot bang of a gun pointed close enough to kill her as her hands ripped Gina's head from her body. She shot out of bed, wide awake, forgetting again.

In the bathroom mirror, she noticed for the first time, the blood on her mouth and hands, the cut skin that appeared to cover her completely. She felt her torso burning and lifted her shirt to find herself spotted with fresh scorch marks cooked into her body. She retched and scrubbed her hands and mouth free of the dried blood. The sight of the red water dripping from her mouth caused more purging of a high-end meal and even more blood. She rinsed her mouth with saltwater, and showered off the remainder of the blood, the water soothing her sores and bruises yet taunting the cuts.

She ordered an at-home STD testing kit for the blood, too afraid to see a doctor in her condition. The commotion outside her window had grown. Emergency vehicles were always around. Cops in the complex from time to time, but this time, even the news was on the scene, as she could see looking out the window. Traffic and onlookers crowded at the sight and smell of what appeared to be a hundred or more dead bodies lying in the road just outside of Deana's bedroom. Channels 6, 12, and 8 were all present and reporting. She assumed a story this big would be live and turned on the TV.

It was not only live but continuing from hours before:

"I'll say that again" the reporter spoke. "B.R.A.D, – Biochemical Research and Defense– that is, arrived early this morning alongside funeral home hearses, and ambulatory services to reclaim cadavers for morgues, schools, hospitals, clinics, and the like. B.R.A.D suspects this is an isolated act of Domestic Terrorism. Perhaps a warning of the threat of magical beings without orders aimed at the non-magical population. The agency will continue to investigate to be certain, but they do not suspect the bodies to rise again.

"However, a small cluster of the bodies appears to have found their way to a local nightclub where there was an attack on civilians, leaving five dead. Some of whom were suspected of running a Rezestra induced prostitution ring. B.R.A.D speculates the attack is a result of a deal gone wrong. Owner of Siren, Angel Cardoza Herrera, and owner of Mynx, Marjorie Nielsen both found among the victims, Nielsen herself was decapitated.

"There appears to be no apocalyptic contagion that spread to those who were scratched and bitten, but B.R.A.D thinks that the dead had help at the scene. Another anomalous character may have aided in the killing of some of the victims as many of the bites and scratches seemed to supersede human capabilities. Possibly the same individual that disturbed the bodies in the first place. More on that as it unfolds. This has been Solana Summers reporting live for channel 8. Now back to Jim Rivers in the studio."

Deana needed to see the damage done at Siren, not remembering her dreamy recollection, but aware of blood on her hands. She flipped to channel 6 and then 12, but each outlet agreed that the images were too violent and graphic to share. Memories tried to return, massive hands holding a shrunken Gina in them, pulling her apart. She turned off the TV and closed the window.

☐

Before Parker knocked, Deana felt them on the other side of the door afraid for her, feeling powerless and more guilty, perhaps for not calling. Another minute passed. They knocked.

"I got here as soon as I..." They noticed her nicked from head to toe and a bruise on her neck in the shape of a gripping hand. "Oh my God Deana!" They moved slightly forward to reach out to her and then stopped.

Deana could feel Parker choking down one fear and a new fear budding. She perceived the two types of terror, both strong, growing from the same root and branching in opposing directions, pulling Parker apart. The bond they shared made the dance almost visible. It was a distinct manifestation, instantaneous, more clear to her than ever before. Parker was afraid for Deana and suddenly *of* her.

Deana was silent for a beat and made herself small trying not to perpetuate their strange feeling. Shrinking as she used to do to keep Laz calm. "What's wrong?" she asked.

"What's wrong with *me*? I should be asking *you* that. You

sounded pretty freaked out when you called. What happened?" They reached for her again and stepped inside with her, shutting, but not locking the door behind them. She noticed.

"I don't know what happened." Deana started apprehensively, "I was at dinner with the woman from Mynx, Gina, or Marjorie, I guess is her real name. the next thing I knew I was home in bed. Covered in these cuts...." *'And someone else's blood.'* she sobbed. "...and she's dead. I feel like I'm cursed." Parker put an arm around her, but neither spoke for a moment. Deana tried to fight the tears, but her nose ran. She cried and Parker held her, petrified and silent.

□

Parker did not hear a single whisper about Deana in June during their brief tryst and not even the other night as they hooked up once more for old times' sake. She was safe enough to be around with no input from disturbed spirits until she came to the door sliced several times over and panicked. A wash of murmurs overlapping drowned each other out speaking at length about trouble to come if Parker chose not to turn away from what was in front of them.

Parker never wanted the voices to be clear, as their grandmother promised they would someday be. It became habit to leave once the source of the warnings was identified and before the static could clear, but how could they leave Deana now afraid, vulnerable, and alone? How could she be so suddenly dangerous as the muffled and disembodied voices tried to urge?

The warnings did not go away as Deana explained leaving work with Gina. Parker tried to focus on her as she spoke, but the voices in their ears persisted. A word here or there became clearer to them, and they hoped they heard wrong. Deana lay crying in their lap, and one determined voice broke through the confusion, "*Devil*

117

hound!" The exclamation reverberated refusing to be ignored.

☐

Deana could read their horrified mood but wished she could read their mind. She anxiously anticipated being alone, but physical presence or not, Parker was pulling away again. She was already alone. Parker's intensifying apprehension set them both on edge. Deana put them out of their misery.

"I was thinking, maybe I rushed it with us before," she began. "I should not have been looking to commit so soon after starting recovery. I've come a long way since then and I don't want to confuse things or get dependent on you all over again. It might be best if we don't see too much of each other." She told them. It was all true, but if not for their feelings she would not have had the strength to resist their company.

"If you think that's best. I probably should get back to the office anyway. I'll check on you tomorrow?" They offered.

"No" Deana started. "I'll be fine. I could really use the time alone to deal with all the crazy stuff I have lived through lately. I'll be back at work on Monday, and I should keep my distance for a while." Deana could sense the gratitude they tried not to feel.

"Maybe we can link up from time to time," they said. "I can introduce you to Mo and her husband, she is rather good with the crazy stuff. You don't have to be alone."

"Okay." She accepted the compromise. "I'll call you." She walked them out before changing clothes throwing on an old tee and faded jeans. Deana opened the locked spare room. From the closet inside she grabbed cans of white paint she did not plan to need until

118

she moved again swapping them with the white crib she hoped to use soon. The soft blue room with it's green, pink, and yellow pastel features were only a reminder that she was still a long way from being a suitable parent.

☐

Friday was therapy. The last if she could help it. Dr. Stevens would have offered the emergency slot, but Deana did not want to go at all. She wanted to forget that she was possibly recalling her own horrible deeds. She wanted to forget everything for a while. She decided against drinking, not certain she could trust herself with even that, though she might allow herself to call Parker eventually, for a more carnal fix, just to keep her from doing something or someone dangerous.

Deana walked into the room and Doctor Stevens could see the tiny scarring all over her. Stevens's inability to hide the concern on her face gave Deana an excuse to respond to what she sensed anyway.

"They don't hurt so bad anymore, as long as I don't move too much," she said and sat.

"I called my girl," the doctor said referring to Deana's boss and her good friend. This time it was Stevens who tried sounding relaxed. "She wouldn't confirm or deny, but I got the feeling you haven't been to work in a while. Are the scars connected to that?"

"You could say that." Deana spared her the details about Friday. She was embarrassed enough not to tell the woman she was right about Laz and how the night got extremely and progressively worse. Alternatively, she filled her in on what she knew about Monday evening. How she came to on Tuesday scarred, shot, and stained with someone else's blood unaware of how she made it home.

"Goodness. I am so sorry. You should have called me sooner."

"Not like there is much I can say. I don't know what happened to me while I was out, but people died. I don't know if..." she shook her head. "... why the bullets didn't rip through me... God what am I?" she put her face in her hands allowing herself to cry again. "I should be put away," she whispered.

The doctor began to wonder what Deana was afraid to say. "Deana, it is a dangerous time to be powerful, but I have been wanting to confess this to someone, and so right now I am going to ask that our doctor-patient confidentiality go both ways." Deana did not respond, but Stevens took a chance.

"I just recently discovered. I can move things, telekinesis, I guess. The first time I noticed, I was running late, and I should have been here by the skin of my teeth, but I forgot that if I am even five minutes off schedule, I will be sitting on a one-lane road behind the city bus. And it happened. Light after light I was stuck complaining and cursing, wishing I could just be ahead of the bus and suddenly me and my car were, *right* in front of the bus. Would have been a blessing had I noticed and kept going, but I was so shocked I didn't move, and the bus driver did not expect me to suddenly be there.

"He had taken on a few passengers and then ran right into me. I felt so bad he might lose his job that I told him I had driven around him on the wrong side of the road and over a median. It was my fault after all. Thank the heavens no one was too badly hurt, but that was the first time I even noticed my ability. I have had to work on patience and practice moving things by desire when I have time off, but maybe I should be put away too if you are."

"You causing a fender bender to a city bus supposed to make me feel better about possibly...?" She sighed unable to say it out loud.

"I only mean discovering new power can be traumatic. Your experience is exceptionally so, but I wouldn't go calling you a killer. It sounds to me like you were drugged. Rezestra maybe, yet somehow you made it home safely. Perhaps you saved your own life. Someone clearly tried to..." She could not imagine. She went on to her next concern. "Most of the discovered mages are people of color and they haven't been treated very fairly. I wouldn't trust just anyone with your story. Or mine. I intend to learn more about the Anomalous and I hope you can trust me to continue to work with you as I do."

Deana shook her head slowly "No, no. I began therapy with big goals...impossible goals..." she paused.

"Not impossible. You've accomplished many of them, Deana."

"Yeah... well now I think I just need to take a break from... *goals*."

"You could always take another semester or two before you–"

"–No, I... I need more time. For school and... everything.

"Everything. Like what?"

"It doesn't matter!" she yelled, "I'm un*fit*! Even this is too much!" Michelle was stunned silent, anticipating. "I *am* on leave from work," Deana continued. "And I just wanted to tell you why I won't be around for a while."

"Now wait Deana, I understand you wanting to retreat after what happened, but it would be best to keep at therapy while you heal, and then we *will* get back on track." It was not optimism, it was begging.

"It's pointless." She insisted.

"How so?"

It was quiet. Then Deana spoke hesitantly, "I've never told anyone... I needed your help when I first came to you. I'd lost..." the dam was breaking. "I thought you could help me... ..."

"What is it, Deana? I'll do anything for you."

The air and sound vanished for seconds too long. Her chest crushed under the weight of the secret held in yet again. She fell backward into herself feeling a sense of Deja vu and a spark of remembrance too brief to seize, but the panic was a noted experience. She jumped up and rushed for the door. Emotions suddenly easy to sort, she felt the pain welling up in Stevens – a feeling like love walking out on her. *Abandonment.* The familiar brand of agony amplified her panic.

"Deana!" Stevens called out to her as she reached the doorway. Sounding professionally concerned, but inside helpless with unrequited love that terrified her. Deana almost felt bad enough to turn around, but she could not bear the woman's feelings coupled with her own. She feared what might happen if she stayed. She left.

Dear reader,

I hope you enjoyed this novella, and I am eager to introduce to you the rest of the family. In fact, for your pleasure, I have included a bonus chapter to further prepare you for the adventures in store.

The following epilogue is an un-proofed A.R.C of a chapter that will ultimately be finalized as part of the upcoming novel in this series. (So… SPOILER ALERT!)

It is an honor to share this with you all. I would appreciate your genuine feedback through private messages on my social medias, but please be kind. To quote Erykah Badu, "I'm an artist, and I'm sensitive about my sh*t."

Thank you, and happy reading,

K. N. Robertson

Epilogue

Parker strolled through the airport looking vacation ready in red and white floral print shorts and matching button up floating open, framing their white tank top; one bag rolling behind and the other thrown over their shoulder. Their short, maple brown curls cut completely off to mark their vacation season. This time, no work. No interpreting, not for dignitaries and businessfolk anyway, though perhaps a little for Monica.

This was a bonding trip, paid for in part by their recent inheritances. The long-separated cousins agreed on Brazil for Monica to fawn over exotic plants and for Parker to meet exotic women at the biggest Pride parade in the world. Parker agreed to translate enthusiastically in exchange for a magic-light trip. They knew magic-free would be too big of an ask. It was impossible for Mo to have Parker's car long without bringing it up in some way, but Parker planned to create an opportunity to present their magical agenda as well.

"Sorry I'm late." Said Parker getting there just after 9pm.

Monica stood to greet them with a hug. "That's okay, I literally got here right before you." They both laughed and she added, "It's great to see you, Nelly."

"Oh wow. No one called me that but Gran, and maybe your mom, but I haven't seen her in years."

"Neither have I."

"You're kidding right? You've been back almost a year."

"I will I just…. You know how it is between me and my mom. Have you given any more thought to my idea?"

"Which idea?"

"Of a coven."

"You could at least buy me a coffee before we go there today. We have all night, you know." Monica ignored the comment, waiting for an answer. "No," they admitted. "I have been trying not to think about that actually."

"You should. We would be so much stronger with a third witch. Hopefully someone with more experience than the both of us, or at least more than you. No offense."

"Good lord…stronger how?"

"We need allies. Power. Something big hopefully. To protect ourselves."

"F-from?" Parker nearly exclaimed.

"I don't know. Other people with power."

They scoffed rolling their eyes letting their head rest over the back of the chair.

Monica continued, "Maybe it's silly, but at least we could have a close magical bond with someone who could teach us, or more likely learn from us in exchange of protection."

Parker couldn't make out any chatter from nearby conversations and proceeded to speak freely not sitting up. "You think we have anything to offer?"

"I think we know a little something that not many people do. No knowledge comes with all the power everyone's been getting lately. I can teach what Grandma Vi managed to get through to me over the phone all these years, and if you come open up those books, then we might really have something."

"Go ahead an open them. You have my blessing."

She hesitated. "I can't."

"Why not?"

"She won't let me." Monica said.

They sat up. "Who?"

Her tone was suddenly choppy and annoyed like a girl of the San Fernando Valley, "Grandma Vi! Who else?"

Parker became impatient too, "What the hell are you talking about?"

"She's got them protected," she explained. "I try to open them, and they won't budge. The covers, the pages, none of them, as if they were cemented shut. Dom can't get them open either."

"And you think I can get them open?"

"She left them to you. I would guess you're the only one who can."

"How in the world did she do that?"

"She might have someone living who is keeping the spell for her, or maybe it's one of those ancestral protection spells. If I knew how to do it, I could probably undo it. I'm sure that's why she didn't teach me that one. Point is if you can open them. It would give us something to offer a newcomer. We can teach them and learn together."

Parker, pensive, used the opportunity to bring up the favor they meant to ask her for again. "I'm sure Deana wouldn't mind being our third. She really could use any help we have, Mo. She's gone through a lot of changes after what happened to her. It's like she's a different person. She's angry and sad and she needs whatever kind of family we can offer her."

"Yeah, I remember you mentioned that. I'll still help her separately. We can share some of the information we have with her, but we should bring someone else into our covenant."

"Covena—" They stammered again, "What's wrong with her? You want a powerful ally. She's got power. If you're gonna mentor her anyway why not have her as close as a coven mate?"

"It's weird. She's your... what, is she?"

"She's my ex, but she's also my friend."

"Ex, slash friend, slash coven mate... you don't think that's one slash too many?"

"She needs the help. Come on. I know you don't like her, but I'll be there to mediate every minute."

"I like her just fine. We're just... different. She's so sensitive. I can't say anything around her without it being a big deal."

"I'll be a bridge between you two, but... maybe we don't call ourselves a coven."

"Mmm, I don't think so. No, we need stay focused."

Parker sighed deeply rolling their eyes again.

"There are other covens, factions, gangs, allegiances. You two together is just too much extra baggage for navigating it all."

Parker's ears perked up at the idea of magical gangs. It was a startling reminder that their newest label meant another fight. Black, Trans, Anomalous.

"A familial third is best," she went on, "but I think we can both agree to rule out any one of our relatives."

Parker grunted affirmatively.

"I drew up a list on my phone of other criteria that combined could help us create a bond with someone else." Monica Passed them her phone.

Parker read the first line out loud. "Assigned female at birth…"

"I thought you might appreciate my correctness."

"I do."

"But doesn't that just sound so mechanical."

"It does, but that's about how it feels to get the assignment at birth, in a way. For example," They put on a phony voice, "This one's a girl! Better get a gun to keep away the boys Mr. Parker. Oh, And this one's a boy, are you going to have him in baseball or football?"

Monica scrunched up her face but chuckled a little. "Now I need coffee. I'm buying. you keep reading." Monica groggily traipsed off to the nearest airport café and ordered two Ethiopian roasts

Parker continued with Monica's ideal candidate requirements and considered them apprehensively: Close in age, African descent, well-educated, spiritual, "Compatible *zodiac* sign?" Parker asked

Monica upon her return. Then more sarcastically added, "Of course, because we wouldn't want our chi's to be out of alignment.

She mocked, "You're so funny today with the jokes." Monica said passing them a warm cup.

"*You* have to be joking." They gave her phone back. "You want us to have our periods synch up too?"

"That's not a bad idea. We are trying to create a lasting bond that transcends time and space. It's a good place to start. We'll need to spend plenty of time together then."

They blinked at her in disbelief. "You were in Cali way too long." They concluded, "Yeah that's it. I think the smog killed too many brain cells."

"If you can suggest a better way to make a connection with someone who isn't family, I would love to hear it."

"Choose someone we know! A friend! Deana! She needs us."

"Okay, we should not bind ourselves to someone out of necessity, number one..."

They said nothing, only stared eyes full of disappointment.

She considered their expression a moment and sighed, guilt ridden. "... What's her sign?"

"Mmm... I don't know."

"How do you not know?"

"That's your thing, Mo."

"Used to be yours too."

Parker grumbled, "Yeah, then I turned eight."

Monica sucked her teeth. "Do you know her birthday?" She asked impatiently.

"Early March. The 4th or the 7th or the 11th."

"Okay, assuming you're right, she's a Pisces." She shook her head. "That explains so much. She's not exactly compatible with either of us. She's a water sign. We're looking for air or fire, like you and me."

"That's insane! She matches literally every other one of your criteria. Down to the powers."

"What can she do again?"

"She's an empath, but … she has another… I don't know. She can tell you better than I can, but it saved her once before."

"And then you got a warning, right? After she mysteriously saved herself?"

They looked away. "Yeah."

Monica got quiet waiting, remembering Parker shut off like this before due to a magical mishap and their relationship had never been the same. "You never told me what you heard."

Silence.

"Are you going to tell me?"

"Not until I figure out what it means and what I can do about it."

☐

131

After 12 sleepless hours, including one layover in Dulles International, They arrived in São Paulo, Brazil. It pained them to say farewell even briefly to the stunning massive city, but they intended to experience it as well before leaving the country. For now, they limited themselves to buying snacks and beverages to settle in for a three-hour bus ride through mountains to São Sebastião and a long wait for a short ferry ride over to the breathtakingly beautiful island of Ilhabela.

"It means 'Beautiful Island,' right?" Monica asked.

"Right." They sounded proud of her when they asked, "Someone's been on Wikipedia, huh?"

"They really don't get enough credit." The hours passed like this gazing, dozing on and off, and cracking one another up by making light fun at each other's expense, the way it used to be.

They arrived at their first bed and breakfast. An underwater coral themed apartment trimmed in white and gold, in a town sandwiched between forested mountain peaks and clear blue water breaking against a narrow shoreline that seemed to be waiting for them to arrive. It would have to wait another day. They each showered and went to bed hungry for an authentic Brazilian meal and eager to explore.

Monica woke Parker up at 6 AM too excited to sleep long. They hopped out of bed already dressed. They'd gotten up around 3AM and began getting ready then finally dozed off again after an hour. Monica caught up by slathering herself in the recommended bug spray they'd gotten at the bus station convenience store to avoid bites from insects that like to leave you pinpricked and dripping blood. They both dressed in swimwear and an outer layer of light material, and headed out on foot to the nearby beach just in time to see the sunrise. It was them and not many others out on the bright day and they'd opted to walk until they could get another taxi to an area with food and refreshing drinks.

They found themselves at a restaurant in a glamorous beach shack. They sat at a table shaded by an umbrella and sipped rum and dined on fresh island fruit taking in the view, still unable to believe nature's ability to create such beauty. Waves continued to embrace the shore and they were two of few around to take it all in.

After eating on this side of the beach they walked on over hills on and off the trail to more private beaches that sat nestled in forests and almost void of any other human life. The two of them removed their trekking shoes and splashed in the cool water. The mood was almost too good to damper. Monica took the opportunity to ask, "Do you still hear the voices when you see her?"

For a moment Parker had forgotten their worries captivated by the serenity of the water slowed by boulders and home to birds of many colors. Their shoulders sagged just a bit as they recalled. "It's just whispers now." They spoke carefully, "This is going to sound crazy, but just hear me out… the voices can tell that I've chosen to ignore them for now," They tried gauging her reaction, but she was still. "At least where it concerns her."

It sounded crazy to her, but Monica was good with crazy. Her voice was calm, but her words still sharp, "Why would you ever do a thing like that?"

"I'm saying," they started in minor defense, "I feel like there's time." They explained more to themselves than her. "Before, the voices always warned of present danger… mostly, but this time, it feels like something is coming… maybe after her. I can't hear it, but I get the energy." They nodded to themselves with a far-off look, remembering, then looked back at Monica, still nodding. "She's in danger. It just hasn't shown itself. I don't want to put us in the line of fire, but she doesn't have anyone at all, Mo. And you said it yourself we have access to information that no one else does."

She pointed a wet finger. "*You* have access to information that no one else does."

"Fine," They threw their hand up, "You want me to say it? I'll admit I need your help too; whatever you can teach me." She looked confused and they continued, "I don't want to learn it, but I'm scared not to. And I don't know what will happen to Deana if I leave her to fend for herself. I always run when the voices start, but they aren't telling me that I have to. And this time is the first time I feel like I shouldn't." They hoped for sympathy, "Come on Mo, you know I can't begin to do this without you. I can't even admit what I can do to anyone. If you didn't know first-hand..." They shook their head wanting to forget again, tears welling up in their eyes.

"I haven't seen you this sure about anything in a very long time."

"I'm not sure about a coven, but... I'm sure about helping Dea."

"How do you even know you can help her?

"I don't exactly, but some part of me believes there is a chance. I attribute that feeling to what I can't hear. The voices know I can't consciously hear them, but they keep at it. Maybe on some deeper level I'm comprehending.

"You're really starting to make me nervous."

"You and me both, but it's real."

"I believe you about the voices and them being real, but are you willing to put us both in danger to try to help her?"

"No. I hope I can find a way to help her and keep us out of danger."

"How exactly?"

"The voices get more... lively when the danger is immediate. Well... I can tell that after whatever happened to Deana there were some voices who wanted me to detach from her then." They corrected, "It feels like I've disobeyed a few of them. They may have even stopped speaking to me, but... I know they'd warn me if I were in danger."

Her eyes big with worry she asked, "And what about me?"

"Like I said earlier, I'll be with the two of you at all times."

"I don't like the sound of you obeying or disobeying voices in your head. On the one hand you sound like a certifiable lunatic, but on the other hand, gran was pretty certain it was your given talent, so maybe it's a bad idea to ignore the... angry voices. God, someone's going to hear us and take us out of here in strait jackets."

"You're so supportive." They said sarcastically and a little hurt.

She smirked.

"So will you help her?" they asked with more audible desperation.

"Parker, this is really complicated and dangerous. Maybe we should study up a little longer and then revisit thi–

"No. Mo. seriously. I should have gotten you involved a lot sooner than I did. You haven't exactly been in a hurry to help, either. I'm not blaming you, I got scared and I've been wasting her time, but she's getting worse. I don't know how much worse she can get or what happens next, but I am sure this is a magic problem.

"Okay. Okay. I hear you. I can't promise I'll fix her, but I'll meet with her. We can decide the coven stuff later."

"There *is* no coven stuff without Deana."

"How is that fair?"

"I don't want to be part of a coven at all. I just need you to help her."

"And in exchange, I'm asking you to be in a coven."

"Why do you need me so bad?"

135

"I need to keep an eye out for you, Parker."

"What about protecting your brothers?"

"It's not magical protection that they need, but I look after them too. Plus, they aren't completely defenseless."

"And I am?"

"No, but you aren't exactly working with your powers, are you? Gran wanted us together to head the family because of our gifts… however … subtle they may present. We're more powerful together. Always have been. I already feel more powerful here with you; as soon as my feet touched the sand, and now with the island water in my braids. Plus, having a womb – a direct connection to the divine – just gives us that much more potential than my brothers." She said with her forefinger and thumb set widely apart. "This whole thing is huge Parker. I get that, better than you because you seem to forget it's bigger than us. We can't have just anybody be our third."

"Deana isn't just anybody," they countered.

Monica sat back against a rock. "Of course, I remember you brought her to meet gran. She couldn't stop talking about it. 'Parker's bringing a girl home. She must be special. Parker's friend sure is pretty. Parker must be in love with this one.'"

They blushed angry and embarrassed, "So you know then."

"All too well! Because I also know that you dropped her ass hard not long after that." She impersonated their grandmother again, "'Parker's friend hasn't been by in a while. Parker's single again already, it was nice while it lasted.'"

There was the cut. "Gran said that?"

"Maybe commitment isn't exactly your strong suit, but on top of that you want to bring an ex into your coven? That's running

136

headfirst into a doomed situation, for both of us. And you haven't mastered even the most basic protection charms. I can't have two neophytes dragging me down. I need real allies."

Parker reached their limit, "Well!" They stood up, the clear and shallow water only up to their shins. They splashed back to the nearest boulder where they placed their belongings and began to put sneakers on to their wet feet. "Don't do me any favors. I'll get my books as soon as we get back to the states." They stormed off into the direction of the underwater themed apartment. "You can just keep your all-mighty knowledge and power and go protect yourself!" It was not profane but sounded that way. They turned to face her once more. "Oh, that's right, you don't have any power," then back again the way they'd come.

Monica gasped, jaw agape in offense. She sat fuming for a moment before grabbing her affects and following behind them at a wide distance.

Parker walked fast and hard but only until they were out of her sight. They slowed and listened long enough to hear the water disturbed. They'd pretended to be uncertain of the direction they came from while waiting for the sound of human-sized steps following behind them never once looking back to be sure it was her.

For a time, they walked consciously listening until they felt secure enough in their guess that she was behind them. They started to make a mental list of rationalizations for not turning around to see that she was following and even for insulting her power the way gran made them promise at a young age that they would never do. They realized that no reason was good enough to continue on without acknowledging to her that they knew she was there this entire time. After all they were in a foreign country.

It was in the same moment that they had the thought to tell her that they would never leave her alone anywhere no matter how mad, that they realized the sound of her footfalls had stopped. They froze. The only sounds were the chirping and buzzing of bugs, croaks of amphibians, and a sound like locusts. For a second, that seemed befitting, the birds fell silent.

They turned slowly to see they were in complete solitude. Alone, they called out, "Mo?"

There was no response, they yelled louder, "Mo!" They began to worry they left too wide a gap between them. They rushed back a few yards to an off-trail clearing where she could have easily lost them. They yelled again. "Mo! Hey! Where are you?" They didn't move sure they'd heard her not far behind around this area. "Monica!" They waited, thinking. Trying to remember.

The words were simple, and they should have recalled them quickly, but they'd let themselves forget the *exact* words they used last time that made everything go wrong so easily.

☐

Shanelle Natalie Parker was turning eight. "It is done!" they whispered firmly to the heavens in insistence to the ancestors that they would, in fact, have their favorite cousin back in Virginia for their birthday.

"I just can't afford to fly the family out for a kid's party Mrs. Friedman" Nelly heard Moonie's father say on the kitchen speaker phone. "Even if I wanted to, I can't get away from work right now, but please wish Parker a happy birthday for me. I will make sure Monica calls."

Nelly was not allowed to say the three simple words together, harmless as they were for any other to speak. They had a gift being a powerful messenger with a direct line to the ancestors' hearts, Gran told them, and it seemed, Gran knew everything. That's how she'd explained it back then and warned Nelly not to use the phrase unless she'd okayed it first.

138

Later that day, they were alone and afraid to even ask for Gran's permission. They worried she might say the same thing she always said, "I'm sorry, Nelly, that's too big-a ask." They'd justified it saying that perhaps if they didn't ask for anything else for a long time it would be alright.

They looked up to the sky, not needing to, eyes closed and whispered confidently and specifically to the ancestors, the way Gran had taught them "My cousin Monica will be at my 8th birthday party no matter what! It is done!" They dried their eyes, thanked the heavens by kissing the emblem they wore on their necklace.

They slept the next two nights thankful, smiling, and certain Monica would be present in time for the fun surprises their mother promised for this year's big celebration. They decided not to concern themselves about rather or not gran would know they disturbed the resting souls of the family for a selfish purpose. They hoped that gran would forgive them if they were really good from now on.

When they rose on the third day, the day of their birthday, the house was busy, but the energy was very unexpected. Nelly could hear somber murmuring from the floor below but couldn't make out a word. They looked out of their window to the backyard to see an inflated bounce house waiting for them. They grinned widely and ran down to the kitchen where everyone anticipated their entrance.

Nelly expected breakfast with mom and dad, gran, and Aunt Reesey, with not just her baby boy cousin, but with Monica too. Gran was there, and dad, but mom and aunt Reesey were not and there were no cousins. Not the kid kind anyway. There were older cousins' teenagers and adults without a smile among them.

"Hi baby, happy birthday," Gran greeted, but there was no plate in her hand or at the table. Just the everyday bowl of apples, bananas, and oranges in the ornately decorated, but chipped, ceramic bowl.

For a moment Nelly assumed that Mom wasn't yet back with breakfast for everyone, and that their aunt was just fashionably late. "Hi everybody," they spoke so grandma wouldn't tell them they were being rude. No one spoke, but a few lips managed to turn up into half smiles.

"Come in the other room and let me talk to you for a sec." Gran ushered them into a front room that no one would really sit in uninvited. Then they knew something was wrong. "Where is momma?"

"She… went to visit your Aunty Reesey in the hospital. It seems that…" she looked up fighting a tear. "Give me strength lord," she asked. Nelly feared the worse, and they were half right. "Last night, someone shot your Aunt Sherice." There was barely a pause, "She's alive and your mother is waiting for her to get out of surgery. All we can do now is wait and pray."

Nelly began to bawl uncontrollably.

"It's gonna be alright baby. I know. I know it's worse, this being your birthday. We hoped you would sleep til we knew she was alright."

It was another 3 hours before anyone knew she was alright. "Your mother says Reesey is up and talking! She is insisting that they come home and celebrate your birthday. Can you believe that? Your mom and cousins will be here any minute!"

"Cousins?"

"Oh, that's right, in all the commotion, I forgot to tell you Moonie's father had her fly in last night with her stepmom and her kids. Your uncle couldn't make it, but Monica will be at your party after all! Which is still on by the way. Only difference now is we get to celebrate your birthday *and* Aunty Reesey's life being saved. Blessed be heavenly God! Amen!" She began to chant and shout praise as she started cooking, but Nelly was left remembering again the declaration they'd made to the heavens. Moonie made it to

Virginia in time for the party, but in exchange, Nelly had gotten her mother shot.

Nelly cried in their room for a short time and when new voices entered the home, they knew it was time to face the music. They snuck around a corner listening before they entered this time.

They heard their mother speaking. "She couldn't even open her eyes yet and she says, 'Monica what you doing here? Get yo ass to that party. And make sure your grandmother saves me a piece of cake!'"

Before Nelly could run in and steal a hug from their mom, before they told anyone they caused this, they heard another voice behind them.

It was a little, but matter of fact voice. "She's okay now. The doctor fixed her."

Nelly turned and their little cousin Moonie was there, sounding sharp as always, but with a new, adult teeth growing in having not completely booted out the baby ones. She was awfully spritely considering the circumstances.

Nelly was quiet, shocked, and unaware of where to begin. Their eyes became glassy.

"I told Gran-gran not to be mad at you if you made it happen."

"You did?"

"Yeah, I know how bad you wanted me to come. I was mad at first, but mommy's not mad. And she's in a really good mood. She said we should try to have fun."

"I don't know if I can have fun."

"Me neither, but we can have cake and ice cream, at least."

141

Grandma Vi talked to Nelly later that night while they helped her finish loading the dishwasher.

"You've been real quiet all night. I think I know why." She said looking down at them out of the corner of her eyes. She kept scrubbing the sink with a dishcloth. She spoke quietly "Did you ask the ancestors to get Monica here for your party?"

They responded barely audible; eyes fixed on the last plate they placed. "Yes ma'am."

She breathed deep and spoke more sternly, "You understand why I told you never to use that gift without me to supervise you now, don't you?"

Even quieter this time, "Yes ma'am."

She started slow, "All the years I have been on this Earth, I wished I had children more powerful than me. My prayer was answered with you, my first grandbaby. Then I wondered why, in all creation, would such a dangerous gift be given to such a small child? Then, I thought, If I knew all the answers then that would make me God. And I don't claim to be. So, I watch and pray you listen when I tell you that some things are just too big to ask for. A lot of things." She sighed hard.

"I spent all night thinking my baby girl would die and on my Nelly's birthday. I put it together but didn't want to believe it. I am glad I decided against asking you then. It gave me the time to be patient enough to hear wisdom. From where I don't know, but as I sat remembering my daughter's life, I realized, her choices made your wish easy for the ancestors to fulfill." Nelly looked up at her. Not sure where she was going.

"The person who shot her is someone she chose to have in her life and then chose to wrong and no matter what you asked for, you couldn't make that happen the way it did. Then I thought longer, over my life… I know my daughter, and I know my granddaughter. I should have known that you would not be able to resist praying for little Moonie to be at your party. I should have seen it coming." She

142

dropped the cloth into the sink. She put her hand on her hips and walked out of the kitchen shaking her head. Nelly knew she was fighting tears. They were too.

Grandma Vi didn't bring it up to Nelly again but repeated the same sentiments at least once more to Aunt Reesey in a slightly less gentle way. It was as close as either of them would get to a real scolding and ten times the power. Nelly hadn't used the gift ever since, and Aunt Reesey hadn't changed much for the better, but she has never been shot again since.

□

Monica heard the first time. She was coming right back, she told herself. They hadn't bothered to look back at her once in all this time, so she figured, losing them for a minute while she stopped to pee was okay. Better than okay, it was what they earned. When they got to the clearing, she remembered that it would branch. They'd go one way, and she could pick from a multitude of directions, handle her business, and get back to the clearing knowing exactly which way to get back to them.

They sounded a little worried around the third call. She wasn't sure how she'd make her presence known without words. Maybe they'd see her and yell at her for not responding, but she was heading back and a touch too proud to go back on her silent stance.

She heard them yelling her name a lot more panicked than before suddenly. Calling like they were no longer worried, but terribly afraid. it sounded like they needed her. She could see them now squinting through tree trunks that surrounded the shaded area. They looked safe, but they still hadn't heard her approaching. She got to them. They were fine physically, but for a minute they were eight years old again. Their pronouns assigned and going by their first name rather than their last. "Parker!" Monica yelled only two feet away.

Seeing her before them as an adult brought them back to the present. They shirked away, quickly erasing the look of terror. They stood seeing she was fine, and they were fine. They started to speak but didn't. Silently, they began walking again. This time staying close to one another. They hardly walked more than two arms lengths apart for the remainder of the trip.

☐

Back at the room they were talking again. Almost normal, but they did not talk about magic, and they did not exactly apologize. Parker offers to treat to their first official authentic Brazilian dinner. They hit the beach again and followed the lights into a lively area of the island for dining, drinking, and dancing with the locals. The dramatics of the afternoon were forgotten and by the time they returned to their B & B, they realized they should have done less partying and more resting up for their big hike the next day.

They started the next rising having another big breakfast and after loading up they sat for a while enjoying the fullness in their bellies and the sound of water breaking against land. After a half hour Monica got antsy, ready to hike the island looking for rare plants on the way to Praia do Bonete, Bonete Beach.

At the start of a very long trail that made up only a fraction of their route, they waited. It was 10AM when Carina met the cousins. She was a local and a well recommended guide for the area. Many tourists came to see animals, some like Monica had even come to fawn over the local flora, but for those who desired to know the magic of Ilhabela and its surviving species of ancient vegetation, only Carina or one of her relatives would suffice as a tour guide.

Her family followed the traditions that survived of the Yoruba culture in Brazil, but they have also found a way to blend it into their modernized Ilhabela life. She was a tall and curvy woman with a heavy base. She wore the front of her hair covered in a blue scarf and spoke some English but was delighted when she learned Parker spoke Portuguese beautifully.

She wore a pink stone that appeared to be magical and eye catching. She led them through trails and off trails to learn of local plants and their medicinal properties. She pointed out birds of many varieties and even showed them where a family of lion tamarins frequented. They heard them, but they swung by too fast to spot.

Parker interpreted for Monica. She captured much of the flora on camera and recorded Carina's teachings for the small community that followed her scientific blog. Carina spoke of the legends and magic cautiously as if she weren't sure it was safe to imply that she believed it to be true, but Monica listened believing wholly.

They stopped at a stream to snack and Carina told of a native legend about a dead man being carried here. According to the lore, this place was chosen as his final resting place only for him to come alive and ask those who carried him for a sip of water. Parker then found the nearest cliff overlooking open waters and jumped in, bathing in the Água da Saúde, Water of Health.

They stopped once more at each waterfall to cool off and reapply mosquito repellant. Besides the *borruchudos* and snakes they really enjoyed the adventure and off-road experience that the hike allowed.

At the final waterfall en route to Bonete Beach Carina stopped to take another dip and Monica used her phone to get photos of flowers and plants. Carina was out of listening range. So Parker asked Monica, "How about Deana is our third and we all look for another person with more ability who can join us. It could only make us stronger, right?" Parker suggested.

"It's actually better to grow a coven by threes. If we look for a fourth, we'll want a fifth and sixth before making it a binding covenant. We should establish our perfect third, first and foremost. And as soon as possible. But all the more reason to teach her as well. We could expand eventually."

"I don't know." They replied, hope suddenly lost from their voice.

Monica wanted the truce to last a bit longer. "We don't have to worry about that today. Let's live it up, one more magic free week and then, when we get back home, we'll get to the books and Deana and figure out the labels or lack thereof later."

"Story of my life. Sounds good to me." Parker stayed near Monica. "I'm sorry I said you don't have power. That was…"

"Not far from true," she finished not looking at them, but at the plant she just photographed.

"Still…"

"Forget it." She continued, "But you know, I don't accept that you fear your powers."

"Pardon?"

"You just jumped off a cliff into some not very deep water and brought your proud, trans ass to Bra*zil*… for *vacation*! You aren't afraid of anything. And you know better than anyone how powerful a bit of knowledge can be. It can save Deana, but it might save you some day too. You're the bravest person I know, cuz. You overcome what happened back in the day, and we'll really see what you're made of."

Intrigued, "Is that a challenge?"

"Damn right it's a challenge."

Parker smiled lightening up tremendously at the friendly competition. Monica was right, they had been quite adventurous, so why stop now?

"See if she'll take a picture with us." Monica said.

"You know, I usually charge for this much interpreting" They replied.

"Puedo... hacerlo... bien en español." She retorted in Spanish and stuck out her tongue.

Parker snickered.

"Is that your subtle way of saying I'm bringing up magic too much on this trip?" They didn't respond. Carina had stripped down to a golden colored bikini that blended with her tanned skin, and stepped into a shallow area of water as if she'd come for a routine ablution. It seemed she'd forgotten about Monica and Parker a moment.

"What's the story with you and Deana anyway?" Monica asked. It was a needless reminder.

"No story, we dated before for a bit, and everything was..." They smiled big, miles away suddenly, "good. Real good."

"Then what happened?"

"... I messed it up. I wasn't ready to commit to her."

"So, you guys are committed now?" She quickly followed Parker's line of sight to Carina again. "How's that going?"

"No, she says she won't commit now. She doesn't think I'm all in. And I guess I'm not, but I want to see more of her, and I know she ain't seeing nobody else." Just then Carina looked up and caught them watching. She smiled, sweet but confident.

"Are *you*?"

They mocked her pitch. "*No*." Then normal, "I haven't been, but I stopped seeing her last time I left the country... she isn't expecting much different from me this time. I did promise to call when I get home though." Carina let herself drift slowly back into the flow of the water, not taking her eyes off Parker, an invitation.

"Lucky girl." Monica said flatly. "Well, I'm asking for a bigger commitment than that; a *binding* covenant."

"Yeah, you mentioned that." Finally taking their eyes off Carina they asked, "You want blood?"

Her face screwed up, "God, no! I guess we could do a shared spell or something. But let's say Deana did join. *Both* of you have to be willing commit."

"Hold that thought…" They walked over to where Carina was wading. Monica shook her head and got back to the plant species she was observing.

When Mo came into earshot to interrupt the giggling, Parker switched to English and loudly asked Carina what her sign was. She understood and answered, "Aries."

"That's good news, Parker. It should be fun while it lasts. She's a better match for you than your ex." She smiled.

It could have been an awkward moment, but Carina asked something in Portuguese.

They tell her they are a Gemini

"Oh my goodness!" she exclaims in a rich accent. "Minha tia-avó é geminiana! Ela diz que Virgem e Gêmeos são os mensageiros dos anjos. Ela tem o dom de saber."

As Carina spoke their smile dropped. "Her aunt is a Gemini too. She says Geminis and Virgos are messengers of the Angels." Parker hesitated knowing Monica would want to hear it more than they wanted to say it, but they were a world-renowned interpreter. It didn't matter if they wanted to say, they would. "She has the gift of knowing."

"Clairsentient?" Mo asked.

Carina recognized the word, "Sim!"

☐

"It's the perfect spot for a photo." Monica said excitedly not knowing it would be one of the last she took on the island. "I can feel it. This one is going to get over a thousand likes."

The three of them stood side by side on a rock-hard path. Monica stood in the center reaching out far as she could to capture all of them and the waterfall rushing in the background.

It wasn't good enough for her. "We should have done a video."

Parker groaned.

"I know, I know, one more." She said, "Just a couple seconds I swear, she said reaching out again." She began greeting the camera lens and monologuing about where they were.

A young guy sprinting by whom they almost didn't notice veered a bit too close. The three of them had eyes fixed on the lens. Carina noticed just in time to yell, "No, no, no!". The man snatched the phone from Monica's hand. She could feel the grazing of his rough pinky knuckle against the thumb side of her hand.

"Hey!" she yelled breaking into a run. "Come back here with my phone!" After only a few steps, his hand lost its grip on it, and it flew backward. She reached a hand up, and caught it, amazed for an instant, then looked up at him again. His expression astonished and mortified. "Yeah." She said barely audible to him from where he stood. Then she yelled ferociously, "You don't want to see what else I can do!" He lingered still in shock. She bucked at him. He ran off. "That's right! Tell your friends!"

She stopped the video capture to get one more group photo. This one even better. It showed an amused Parker, a delightfully surprised Carina, and Monica glowering with pride, grinning ear to ear.

☐

The tour lasted almost the entire day, but it was unquestionably worth every step. At sunset, the tour guide led them to a dock, and they rode back in a small fishing boat that dropped them near the restaurant where they ate earlier. They would have gladly had dinner there as well, but Carina invited them to party with her family. "They used any excuse to celebrate, and the elder women would have been cooking all day," Parker translated casually, their mind too tired for formalities. "Tomorrow Carina is traveling to São Paulo for the Pride Parade."

She added in English, "My cousin Danny and his friend got to work on eh... Carro Alegórico."

"Allegorical car?" Said Parker.

"A float!" said Monica.

"Sim! A float. We have been invited to ride along. You two should come. We're taking the ferry back to São Sebastião early, then meeting up with a friend who has a van. It'll be crowded, but you won't have to wait for the bus."

Monica was delighted. The cousins agreed that it could be the perfect opportunity to have a more genuine experience their last night on Ilhabela. It was another hike finding Carina's car. She drove them to a favela carved into mossy peaks and valleys. In the distance the water could still be seen. That and the billowing foliage were the only distinguishing factors between this barrio and any other city in the world they had seen.

They parked on a side street and walked up a hill of bricked pavement past a local pizzeria to get to a raised pink house full of life and smelling of roasted pig. Her big close-knit family, inside as she said, cooking. They also danced, drank, cursed, laughed, cried, and fought. The place alive with people of all ages, music, and an old woman in a coral-colored headwrap and a shelled necklace who stared at Monica or Parker.

"She wants to talk to you both," Carina told them. She knows of your powers, but I promise I did not tell her." They hadn't considered rather or not they believed her. Parker was unsurprisingly apprehensive, but even Monica shuffled toward the woman anxiously. Neither of them daring to refuse her.

"Boa noite," Parker started, but she was uninterested in customs.

The woman spoke hurriedly as if they needed the message quickly. Parker translated as best they could, speaking as if the words were their own, but the wave of mysterious wisdom regarding them was agonizing.

"The mistakes of the last two generations will be healed by the triumphs of the next two," they said. "The responsibility to take on this fight has come to you.

"One specific ancestor favors you." The woman was speaking to Parker, but they continued to interpret. Monica watched mesmerized. "They have earned you a path to your other ancestors and they understand your choice to ignore them, but it is not Deana that they are warning you away from." They shivered hearing the woman say her name so confidently.

"There is another with great ability who will need you in order to shift the fate of the world to its best chance... But you need her if you are to pick up here your ancestors left off - in a battle of a war that is not the fault of those who must resolve it."

"How can we stand a chance in this war?" Monica asked. Parker was stunned by her calmness at the absurd message, but they interpreted without a pause.

The elder woman pondered, and the answer came. "Não confunda consequência com maldição." She said eerily.

Parker stared at the matriarch as they received her words in confused horror. "Don't confuse consequence with… curse?" They said.

There was a hush in the room, even the music paused. She continued with another late arriving message for Parker to relay. "Your perfect coven is four," they translated.

Monica spoke again when she heard. "Pardon me, but I believe covens of three or multiples of three have better harmony and fortitude."

Parker began translating. They were still speaking when the woman interrupted. "Seu coven perfeito é quatro!" Monica didn't need it translated this time. She let it go for now. The woman continued with a final message. Parker didn't speak.

For a moment, Monica was the only one in the room who didn't understand. "What did she say?"

"I…" They said nothing.

"What?"

"She said if we don't find our fourth by the time the big storm clears, then we may not have the chance to keep the advantage."

"What storm?" Monica asked.

Parker considered, they shook their head, shrugged. "Desculpe-me" they bowed to the woman respectfully and walked out.

"Parker?" Monica said.

Carina began to follow them.

"It's okay," Monica started. "I got it."

☐

Parker spoke first. They were just outside of the front door, pacing in paradise feeling like there was nowhere to run. "I'm tired, Monica."

She hoped they weren't too far over the moment for her to make light of it. "I really wasn't going to bring up magic again on this trip. Not even after I got my phone back, which was *huge* for me by the way, but fate, aided by your hormones lead us here. I know you don't believe in coincidences."

There was raucous silence. They didn't find it funny.

"Well, if we aren't going to talk about magic," she shut her eyes tightly, relieved to confess, "then I no longer have a proper distraction from the thoughts that tell me Dominic is having an affair."

Parker stared at her; eyebrows raised at the shock of her gall. She continued, "I don't have any proof, but that's just making me more paranoid. He says he's working late all the time, he's out before I get up for the day and in long after I go to bed at night.

"He's sleeping somewhere. I don't know what else to think, so I stay busy. Otherwise, I will have to confront him. I'm just not ready. If he says he isn't cheating, I won't believe him, and if he says he is, I'll kill him... Forget I said that."

Parker looked uncomfortable but sympathetic.

"Well, we came here to bond." She shrugged.

"I don't know what to say. Wish I could tell you he wouldn't cheat, but I barely know the guy."

"Yeah, I know. She looked down."

"We can talk about magic I guess, but... I can't even think about what Carina's aunt just said. Anything but that. Please."

"I don't know why you're so surprised. Not like gran hadn't already told you most of that."

"What? Gran never told me any of that."

"Well, she didn't know the specifics to that extent, but she's been talking about the war for a long time. She didn't call it a war either, but I think she just didn't want to scare us. Gran called it our 'inherited work' and our 'legacy;' sugarcoating. She's the one who said it as bigger than us."

They massaged their temporal lobes. "Great."

"I can't believe you – the pride of the family - don't know any of this."

"Me? You were always her favorite."

"No way, you're the one with the great power," she mocked a mystical voice. "She'd been waiting on you all her life. When you stopped practicing, I thought I could at least be the one with the information, but she left you the family tomes. You're the one who's always shown power and I spent my whole life trying to catch up to the chosen one from the other side of the country. Why do you think gran and I talked so much? She was trying to catch me up to you! Long distance calls weren't cheap back then either."

"She left you the house."

"Yeah. Guess she wanted us close. Wouldn't have happened if she divided it up the other way around."

"You would still be in California."

"Yeah, but I'd still have to find two more coven mates no matter where I live. How the heck am I supposed to make a connecting factor with a coven of four? Four is not the magic number! "She was flustered for the first time this trip. "It's stable enough I guess, but... how do we know if stable enough is stable enough? You know?"

"Yeah, we're just barely stable enough just the two of us." Parker joked. They were beginning to loosen up.

Monica managed to chuckle but remained tense. There was a quiet moment except for a few lively voices in the distance.

"Mo, why didn't you get mad or make me feel bad when you found out that it was my manifestation that got your mom shot?"

"Wow. Been sitting on that one a long time, have you?"

"Someone told me I might be something if I get past it."

Ironically, she smiled. "Adult me knows you wouldn't have made the wish if you'd known my mom would get shot. But back then... well... I remember leaving the hospital to come to your party and I kept thinking... my mom had never been nicer to me than when she was lying in a hospital bed. That is still one of the finer moments in our relationship. I think that is around when I realized she loved me. She didn't say it, but... the first thing she said when she came to, was about me. That's all I knew. I kept forgetting to be mad. I was too happy knowing she cared about me.

155

And she didn't die!" She added rejoicing. "Who would have guessed, my dad spent more than 20 years in the military and my mom's the one who gets shot."

Parker laughed uncomfortably.

"She was okay. And she loved me."

Peace. They were at peace and considerably bonded, but the voices of three roaring men approached. They watched downhill at the figures coming closer to the house. They ascended the hill, now chanting.

"Viva o orgulho! Viva o orgulho! Viva o orgulho!"

It sounded the same as it did in Spanish. "Live the pride?" Monica asked.

"Yeah!" Parker said excited again for the next leg of their trip.

The men appeared drunkenly with scratched faces, chiseled and tan, and shirts stretched and holey. They arrived at the door passing Parker and Monica, facing them inviting them to cheer, "Viva o orgulho! Viva o orgulho! Viva o orgulho!" They continued, Parker and Monica joining in and following behind them back into the house.

Inside Carina greeted him first excited but noticing his scars just before she embraced him. They each began to speak excitedly over one another.

Monica whispered to Parker, "Remember everything they're saying. I want details later." She walked away to finally help herself to a plate. Parker squeezed in to absorb the story Danny told.

It was an attempted hate crime. Thugs causing trouble the day before the parade. They managed to get near the floats hoping to destroy enough of them to stall or prevent the parade all together. One of the louts had a talent he hoped to use for steaming up the

156

engines. He didn't manage to do more than give it a nice clean before Danny and his friends, caught him. A crowed of homophobes blocked the entrance but Danny and his friends were willing to fight their way in to get to the float. He broke his way past and came face to face with the steamer who blew piping hot vapor into Danny's face that whistled from his mouth like a tea kettle. Danny swung a fist blindly and connected with the jaw of the attacker.

He spoke so passionately that Monica felt words were obsolete to the story, but later in the privacy of Carina's hatchback, Parker performed the English version of Danny's story. "They started with the wrong float!" They yelled aggressively swinging a punch with their right fist landing into their left palm, eyes closed. Take that!" They shouted, "and then his friend, the little guy, got in and tackled the steamer to the ground. He wailed on him, and others began to trickle in. Danny's other friend said that a lot of the thugs scattered when sirens started going off around them. The steamer took a few good hits before they let him run off too. But they threw anything they could get at him to make sure he didn't try to blast them again."

☐

They packed up their first room and slept for the time they had, intending to meet Carina at the ferry before dawn. They ferried back to São Sebastião and got a ride in a van full to capacity with the three of them, Danny and his two friends, and another friend of theirs who had gotten them back and forth to the float when they came to help. It was 7 hours before they finally parked relatively near the parade and hiked again in the direction of the festivities.

"There is literally a million people here," Parker said when they'd finally joined the parade from the top of a float.

"More!" said Carina.

One of the other riders addressed the crowd on a microphone. Not all could hear of course, but there was a recap of the vandals who tried to stop the parade from happening. The speaker reminded the crowed to celebrate more charismatically. "They want to force us back into the closet, but we live proudly!" He said in Portuguese.

To which Danny responded, "Viva o orgulho!"

Everyone who heard repeated the phrase, "Viva o orgulho! Viva o orgulho! Viva o orgulho!"

The chant rippled back and back until it couldn't be heard by Parker on the float where it started. A new song began to play loudly, and streets of people danced together. Looking out into the crowed Parker could see one attractive and very topless woman with painted breasts and torso walking, swaying her hips to the rhythm of the music. She strutted watching Parker long before they noticed her. They smiled at her, more out of habit than interest.

Carina noticed them smiling at the woman and with an index finger gently turned their head to face her and kissed them passionately. "Viva o orgulho!" Parker shouted to the crowed afterward with a fist in the air.

Those on the float and in hearing range started again crying out, "Viva o orgulho! Viva o orgulho! Viva o orgulho!" Couples on the float and in the crowd shared a kiss in waves that rippled backward to seal the chant, and it was magic.

☐

It was terribly late and becoming early. They were being driven to their second bed and breakfast in the crowded van, finally checking in and happily exhausted.

Drunk, Parker said, "I forgot how much fun we are together. Always thought it was just because you were my cousin and we were always around one another, but maybe there is something to that Air and Fire thing you were talking about.

"Oh! That's it!" Monica was trashed, but her wheels still turning. "*All* the elements," she said as if it were a complete thought. "Of course!" she said seeing two of Parker. "We're mutable! Two down, two to go."

They laughed in her face. "I have no idea what you're talking about."

After they stopped guffawing, Monica said, "We need a Pisces and a Virgo! It's probably fair we each pick one, and unless you changed your mind…"

"I'll text Deana right now!"

"…Great," she said and there was no sarcasm this time. "But that still leaves a Virgo… Might be hard to find. They are the hermit of the zodiac." She whispered, "I might know someone who knows someone, but…" She looked over to see no one was listening, "Might be easier if you just do that thing you do."

Parker sobered, "I don't do that anymore, Moonie."

"Would be good practice." Monica tempted.

They started to mock "With…" then they recalled the oracle's words "…consequences."